The First Satan
Rise of Yeqon

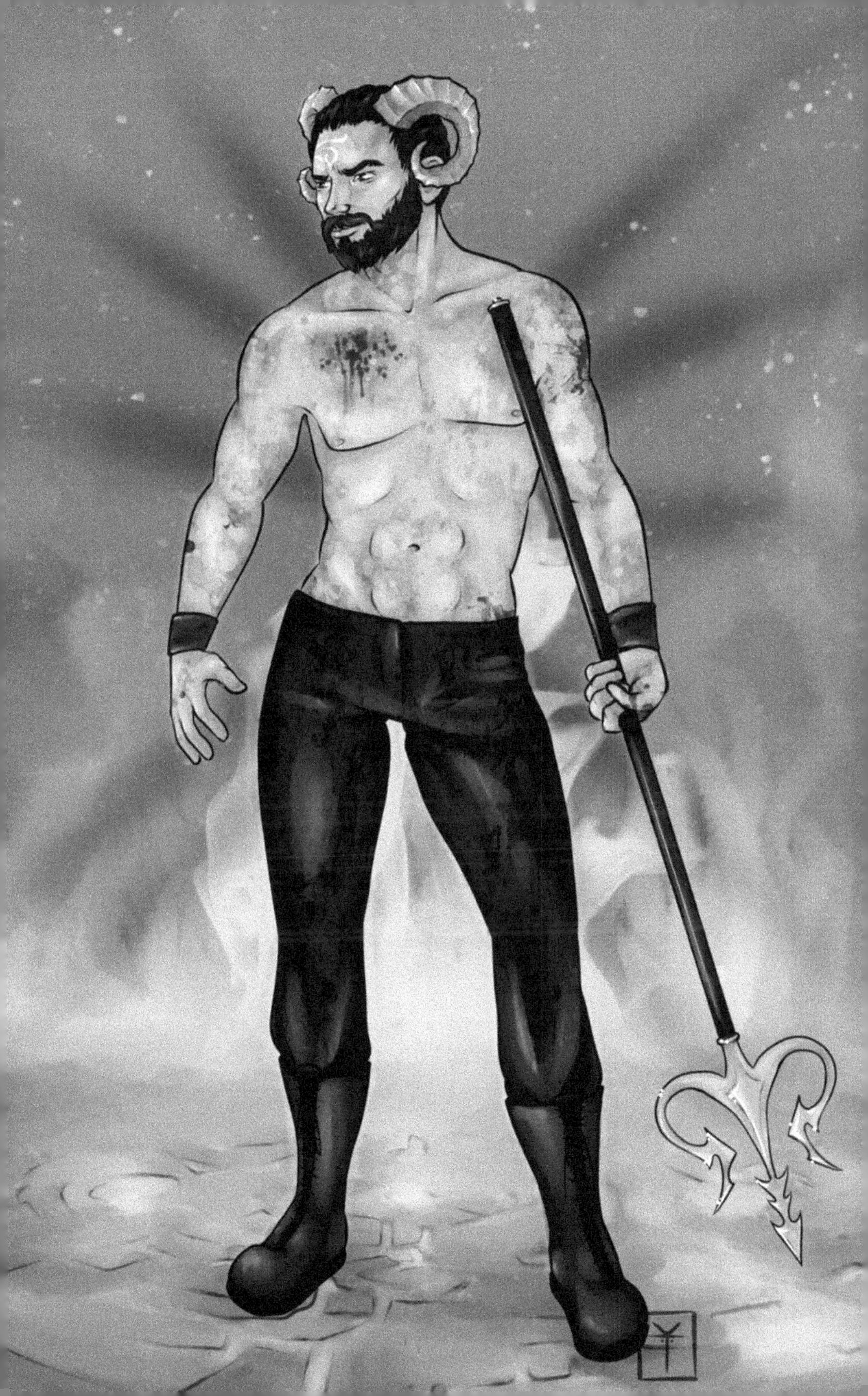

The First Satan
Rise of Yeqon

G.R. Thomas

To my dearest readers, old and new,
Your love of The A'vean Chronicles stirred this story to life.

"Hell is empty and all the devils are here."

WILLIAM SHAKESPEARE

Chapter One

Yeqon hated humans. They occupied his mind night and day, year after year, century after century. He couldn't close his eyes without thinking about them, awoke from every Psynostris sleep cycle with them tattooed on his mind. This day was no different, and it stirred his thoughts of home.

Fingers blackened, he threw a nub of charcoal back into a dying fire pit and admired his unflattering outlining of a human on the paled bark of the tree he had used for his shelter.

"No eyes, for you do not see, no mouth for you cannot speak," he mumbled at the image. He spat at his crude drawing. "You'd be nothing without us." Branches cracked under his bare feet as he made his way around the tree, retrieving a thick, chromious-lined belt heavy with weapons. Yeqon slid three short-bladed daggers out and rounded the tree again.

A gentle breeze sung through the trees; birdsong called in the distance. He shook his head and peered up at a strike of predawn sky, stars still fading.

"This will be the last day, Father, I'll endure another cycle watching them." Yeqon's voice rumbled like a torrent as he spat the warning to I'el, the creator of all things. Yeqon sniffed a short cold breath, closed his eyes as the weapons warmed in his palms. Memories of home, the great world of A'vean flooded his mind's eye. Enormous diamond-hewn homes, the gentle song of waterfalls and endless comforts tended the weariness of his patience. Yet the yearning grew stronger with each passing day, and that patience thinner by the second.

His eyes snapped open. "And now I suffer this." He spat again; it was almost involuntary how Earth made his mortal body react.

Hands now heavy with daggers that glowed with A'vean power, one by one they flew blade over handle until embedded in the human effigy. One in each eye, one in the heart. Yeqon snorted. "If only you screamed," he spoke to the effigy as he yanked his daggers free.

Roosters crowed nearby; a cow bellowed. Footsteps told him the encampment was waking.

"Ugh," he sighed and finished dressing, mindful to let his Pterugia, his wings of light, flex before he had to tuck them away, hidden within his spine, lest they accidently blind an errant human.

He sat upon a rock by the embers of his fire, took a long draught of honey mead and retrieved his sharpening tool. The milky quartz sung as it called a razored edge back to the blade.

The quartz shook in his grip as he ran it along the edge of the chromious sword. He smiled at the way the precious, otherworldly metal purred as he sharpened it. His eyes narrowed as its shine glanced across his face, fading fire light catching the power that coursed within the metal mined only on A'vean.

Nothing like chromious existed on Earth, and Yeqon despised the place for it. The planet needed another million years at least, perhaps another cataclysm to push its evolution, but no, I'el insisted it be tended as is.

Yeqon hated the unpredictability and vulgarity of this planet at the arse end of the universe. Once no more than a speck that didn't draw the eye of I'el, now, it was the centre of everything. The apple of His eye, the meat on His bones, the highest peak of all His creations, and yet, humans couldn't see themselves out of their own shadows without help.

A sigh rumbled in Yeqon's chest. He ran his fingers along the razor edge, winced and smiled when a seam of red ran along his skin.

"It's been too long since you tasted blood, old friend." He lifted the sword and kissed the flat edge of it, breathed in its unique smell, let the power of it hum against his lips a moment.

"You'd like the taste of human flesh." His smile waned and he pushed up from his seat, and held the sword in front of his face. His reflection was warbled, his face contorted, the deep umber of his skin paled in its eye. He probed the silvery markings that curled around his right eye, his Mark of A'vean, a measure of his heritage expressed upon his mortal flesh. It glimmered under the touch of his fingers, angelic energy surging towards their warmth.

"You speak a truth." He let the weapon rest against his forehead, and he felt every bit as twisted as the blade's reflection seemed to infer. The sword sank quietly into its scabbard as he readied himself for another day of tending I'el's greatest mistake… he looked back at the impaled outline of the human.

A warm morning greeted him as he left the cover of the forest, rounding the side of a hill that overlooked the mid-east lands. Hands skimming along smooth rock, Yeqon breathed in and stared across the expanse of the Göbekli Tepe region. A wide valley of sand and rock, interspersed with tree groves, Göbekli Tepe portal stood proud in the middle of a hidden village of A'vean souls. An outpost for those who had run afoul of I'el, for those who had not followed His rules to perfection.

Yeqon's cheek twitched, his eyes narrowed as he took in a scene of beleaguered angels who struggled to find purpose day in and day out… protecting humans. Many lounged by a small river, some practiced war games throughout the trees, others drank their human bodies into oblivion with the boredom. Yeqon's fingers twitched when he saw Belial by the river, fist-fighting another to a pulp. He could smell the rich tang of blood, almost feel flesh squash beneath his knuckles; his lips pulled into a smile. He stepped towards Belial, but felt a tap upon his shoulder, his feet ground to a stop. His brows knitted when he saw who it was.

"What do you want?" Yeqon snarled, knuckles whitening into fists.

"To get this job done and get out of here," Pineme said. His rainbow-coloured eyes rolled skyward. "And the quicker the better, Yeqon." His mouth was tight, eyes thin, scouring Yeqon's face.

"I'el may be silent, but you know He is always watching us. Don't stray Yeqon, that's what got you into this mess." Pineme licked his lips, "It's what got us all into trouble."

Yeqon grumbled, let his hand relax, unable to avoid a quick glance at the clear blue sky.

Nothing. You give me nothing, he thought as he sought any kind of sign from I'el.

"Why are you even here Pineme? Thought you were keeping some other shit hole in order?"

Pineme chuckled, nodded his head, his face a hybrid of amusement and disgust. He clucked his tongue, ran a hand across the wide expanse of his chest. His Mark of A'vean glimmered a little brighter against his brown skin.

"Well, I was until I got too persuasive with the locals of Venlos. By the Throne, they just wouldn't evolve, wouldn't learn, I don't think they *could* learn." Pineme scratched his head, his eyes swirled, the colour rose and fell with his emotions.

"Figured I'd nudge them, figured incorrectly. Caused a whole village to drown, literally." Pineme's brows piqued as his eyes rolled. "Turns out if you push them in a river to get to more fertile land, they don't actually learn to swim, they just sink." Pineme sucked in a breath, rubbed his chin. "Bit like this lot." He jerked his head towards a distant mountain range where the closest human settlement struggled day after day. He laughed, "Of course, there were plenty more Venlayan's, but unsurprisingly, the Throne couldn't see past the accidental deaths... or my impatience." Pineme ground his toes into the hard earth. "Now I'm here to just observe, hands off the locals unless there's an extreme event. Just like you, Yeqon. I'll not get caught out again though, in case I end up somewhere worse than this." He scanned the landscape, a deep sigh whooshed through his pursed lips.

Yeqon glared at Pineme, his eyes rolled over him from head to foot.

Pineme shifted, one foot edged back. He swallowed hard, hands slipping to his belt, hung low with weapons.

"What of Venlos now?" Yeqon asked.

Sweat beaded above Pineme's lip, "It was abandoned."

Yeqon's lip twitched. He nodded; brows still tight.

"Watching, isn't it the pinnacle of existence, that I can assure you of." Yeqon grimaced. "Get used to it, I've been trapped here an age with no sign of release. I'el has forgotten us, just as he has abandoned Venlos, you can be sure he has abandoned our wellbeing." Yeqon released his wings of light, the heat of them wilted the leaves of a low tree branch, the deep green curling into a blackened crisp.

"Perhaps though, there could be a way…" Yeqon's words faded. "I'll be back by dusk." With one undulation he was airborne, banking north west towards the northern henge portal, escape on his mind.

Chapter Two

Yeqon crossed the globe, through the change of season into a bleak, chilled airstream. He focused on the shadow of his body on the clouds below, a blurry-edged grey blot following mindlessly along. That's exactly how he felt, relegated to what he now was; nothing more than a shadow of a great warrior. An equally rage-filled wind whipped at a dark band of his hair that striped through an otherwise silvery length. The weather pushed him up, then down, and he let its anger buffet his body until he cleared the expanse of a wild and frothy ocean, eventually drifting across the island continent he had suffered on a daily basis for more years than he cared to count. He set down in the middle of a thick forest, denser than the mid-east with a feel to it that prickled his skin. The air was frigid with dew, his skin tightened with the bite of frost and he fanned the heat of his wings around his body to dry off.

Yeqon's eye ticked as he tucked his wings away, immediately uncomfortable as the cold resurged against him. The forest spoke, its melancholy chorus of swaying brunches and rustling undergrowth in tune with his emotions. He drew a deep breath, thought momentarily of flying in the opposite direction, but then recalled Pineme's worries.

What if I'el was really watching them? Would He deliver a worse punishment if he strayed again?

"You wouldn't be that interested anymore." Yeqon glanced up, a thick tree canopy obliterated any view of the sky. "Hmm." His teeth ground; he sniffed and spat. Yeqon watched the slimy wad of phlegm ooze down the brown cap of a mushroom… and that was all he ever did… watched like a mindless, purposeless lacky. That's all I'el allowed. His fists clenched as he thought of war, of purpose, of that gut tightening joy of victory. His knucklebones gleamed through his skin, his teeth grated, and he broke a sweat forcing away thoughts of no action, no interference; frustratingly little fist to face, skin to skin, weapon to bone contact.

Yeqon moved silently through the forest, his bare feet sliding through a slimy undergrowth, his sneer deepening as mud squelched through his toes. I'el forbid he flew too close to human settlements and stunned one of them. His dark eyes flitted skyward where the green canopy was thick, where the daylight was mere slashes of cloud here and there. The ground was icy. Leaf litter carried upon a slithering fog, it tried to claw into him, to sink within him. Yet, with every step it shrank away, overwhelmed by the power that burned just beneath his skin. The fog bowed to his presence, folded back upon itself and made a pathway ahead.

A veil of pasty light struck a clearing beyond the tree line. Yeqon turned towards it, an easier pathway towards his charges. A brisker wind whistled through a thousand tree trunks, sucked at the fog, clawed for leaves as it birthed a storm. He stopped in a patch of light streaming to the ground and breathed deep. The forest seemed to stop, take a breath of its own, as though listening in, waiting to see what his next move was. Toes clawed back from a deepening mud, Yeqon peered skyward again, thumb and forefinger rubbing a stubble he'd let grow. Squinting, his pupils narrowed upon an unsettled sky.

Beyond bilious clouds, he wondered if I'el was really watching. Did the creator of all things have the time to focus on what he was doing so very far away from A'vean, the world he was birthed in, the world he called home... the world he yearned for? Yeqon's thick brows twitched, a brief beam of wintery sun struck his skin, a warm slap, then it was gone, cold eagerly settled into its place. His eyelids narrowed further, the rainbow orbs within glimmered a little brighter.

"Is that all you've got?" The chuckle died in Yeqon's chest.

He cracked his knuckles, one hand slipping down to rest upon the hilt of his sword. The familiar vibration of it set the coil of his muscles at ease and he let it course up his forearm until its power shot through his body upon his next heartbeat. The damage this weapon could do on such a planet, slipping through all the human skin yet to be tested made his heart race a little faster and that empowering tingle last all the longer. He imagined the blade sear through delicate human flesh like air, as though nothing at all had glanced upon the powerful weapon. His smile was more genuine now, it pushed his cheeks up a little and the cold no longer bothered him.

His fingers slid from the sword, they twitched, unsatisfied with the lack of war. He turned his hand back and forth, examined the flaxen sheath of skin that held the muscle and bone within. His fingers curled in, cracked, then extended until the veins on the back of his hands bulged.

"Hmph." He sniffed as those veins lit like liquid silver beneath the skin. The fleshy body he acquired when he was sentenced to Earth was at first an annoyance. It felt pain, took longer to heal than his patience tolerated, and it was far too susceptible to the elements. Yet, over time, and through utter boredom, he had come to enjoy the variety of its colours and textures, as well as the pleasant physical sensations when one or more bodies was thrust upon another in certain ways. He licked his lips, his heart raced, and a flush of something distinctly human clawed up his neck. He smiled a little more, eyes glassy, a warmth flushed through his lower half and he groaned. Thoughts wandered, Yeqon ran a thumb and forefinger over the back of his forearm, pinched the skin until it whitened and bruised. He enjoyed the pain, but pain was also the ultimate weakness that controlled humans, as well as this flesh and blood casing he had to endure. His skin cooled, and his mouth sank back into a grimace. He snorted in disgust and spat once more.

Yeqon walked on, the edge of the forest nearer with each unwilling step. He pinched his nose and scowled; the excrement smell of humans assaulted him before they even came into view.

The forest thinned, light chased darkness away and a miserable slice of openness presented itself. Yeqon recalled the shimmer of his veins deep within the meat of his arms, locked his Pterugia snuggly into his spine, and tried to look as human as possible before he stepped out towards the ancient stone henge portal. He hesitated, swallowed disgust as he stared across the land, one hand on a tree trunk, nails biting into its bark.

Despite the early hour, when the birds had barely finished their morning song, humans toiled around the great stones, grunting and yelling; laboured breaths misted into a bleak and colourless backdrop. Two bulking overseers lashed the less enthusiastic, the ones that lagged behind, the ones that dared to look up from their task. A whiskered length of plaited twine swung through the air, its tip coated in blood, old and new. Yeqon smiled again, despite himself, this he appreciated. The warm odour of fresh blood fanned a comforting curl of satisfaction in his belly.

He stood a while, allowing the sun to arch over the horizon, an insipid white orb that lent little to the day other than a muted light. As the morning wore on, the humans toiled harder, faster, and Yeqon watched on in resentful, intolerant silence. He recalled his feelings about humans; an obsessive mantra choroused his thoughts.

Stupid, weak; a plague.

It helped momentarily, but in the end, day after day, there he was, as he had been since the great directive, watching the miserable creatures exist, trying to pull themselves from swamps and caves with little more than hunger and sex to drive them. His tongue ran along his teeth, his teeth sank into his lower lip, and boredom set in, a gnawing tension that teased his power, made his skin shiver.

Yeqon sighed deeply, sneered skywards, then dropped his gaze, looking at his outstretched fingers. They cracked as they flexed, they sounded like the satisfying snap of breaking necks.

"So much more you could be doing," he huffed, one hand falling back to the smooth handle of his sword, the hum of the chromious tingling his fingertips.

"Be damned with it." He turned and stepped back towards the centre of the forest, relishing the enveloping darkness of it. Yet, he only made it a few paces. He stopped, shook his head, fingers twitching for his weapon again. Colour flushed his face, a vein pulsed angrily on his temple and his Mark of A'vean shimmered underneath his skin.

He groaned, then yelled, his voice reverberated into the forest depths, bringing it to life with fear as birds scattered, and things in the undergrowth scurried away.

He turned back towards the stone henge, the warrior in him frustratingly bound to finish a directive, adherent to I'el, however unwilling. He grumbled like a juvenile soul, one newly birthed from the Milacean mountains of A'vean. Begrudgingly, he followed the trail to the edge of the forest.

Yeqon settled under a clutch of Blackthorne trees and stared across the fog-choked plain. Human workers still toiled on, there were more of them now as the day evolved. He counted fifty around the perimeter of the henge, perhaps another hundred in the immediate vicinity forging tools, stoking fires for food and warmth. He watched on as they struggled to repair the great henge portal. It was older than time, a thing of great mystery to the humans; simply a mere interstellar route for A'vean souls.

Revering the great Watchers, it was a labour of love for humans, a task set in place in their dreams eons ago. Gentle murmurings from the shadows that the Eloi, the first five Watchers, imbued upon humanity, the first spark of intelligence, the first push towards purpose. Yeqon recalled their wide eyed wonder when the spark of self-awareness hit them. When a knowing, a deep subconscious urge drove their predecessors to pick up a stick and rub it against another. He recalled the moments their guttural grunts softened into the threads of oral language. All because the Eloi and himself gave them the spark, set a thread of knowledge weaving within the depths of their thoughts. These enlightenments gave humanity a reason to evolve, to pull themselves from the swamps. This knowledge however, stoked something unexpected… greed and a sense of entitlement.

Yeqon sighed, picked his nails clean with his shortest dagger, and settled against the nearest tree to do what he did best these days… merely exist.

Hours passed. The humans, to their credit, did not give in to adversity. The task was immense, the idea of tending the stone portal a driving force that became a faith. Yet, in that faith, despite sheer brute strength, they struggled. Despite those early nudges, intellect eluded them, they failed to adapt, to learn, and those great stones injured and maimed hundreds. Yeqon let it happen though, let fate have its way as I'el had intended, as He had commanded.

Yeqon did not interfere, but with each hour, with every long day, with every passing moon cycle, a gnawing tension infected him; it scraped under his skin like an itch that could not be scratched. A'vean power burned beneath the surface, made his mortal body uncomfortable, too tight to contain him. Yet he watched on, a shadow, a dream, humanity none the wiser.

Chapter
Three

The stone henge remained broken for an age. The portal it powered was unreliable, its light flickered on and off, its path to the stars unsafe. A'veans were still unable to transfer to the region with ease, and that made Yeqon's job all the harder. He was supposed to subtly urge the humans to fix it quickly. His skin sizzled at the ridiculousness of it. He could fix it, any of them could, but the humans *had* to learn by trial and error according to nature's law, and as he thought on the past months… there'd been an eternity of error and not a lot of help from nature other than the weather that hindered them.

Of course, Yeqon had asked for support from I'el, but received silence as a response as usual. This north western portal was integral as the most direct thoroughfare to A'vean, where the other portals were set to regions in universes much further away. It was therefore imperative the doorway to his homeland was clear and always open.

Yet, help was not given, the others suffering their fate on this forsaken planet had their own directives, none of which involved helping him. It was just Yeqon's wearied eyes upon the repairs, and it wasn't happening fast enough for the impatient grind in his bones. They needed more A'veans on Earth to manage an ever growing human population, an infestation he personally felt should be halted until they were more evolved, more capable of surviving to maturation without succumbing to simple maladies. Yet, Yeqon did as he was ordered.

As the day wore on and the sunlight faded into a starless, inky smudge, Yeqon bided his time until it was safe to assess the progress. Upon a waxing moon, his wings released with a soft hum and he groaned with the pleasure of the relief. His feet lifted from the icy ground and he breached the cover of the forest. He moved in, the blanket of night his opportunity to discover how much longer he must suffer this assignment.

Yeqon flew in covertly, a shadowed figment in the dreams of the humans far below. He circled the portal, settled gently upon the central altar stone. The portal's power stuttered, blinking white against the night sky.

"Hmmm," his muted groan belied the scream of frustration that sat like a stone in his chest. The great stones of the henge hummed under his touch, the erratic power comforting when it generated a momentary burst to the heavens. Its white sheets set the night ablaze, a flickering tease towards home. Its power stirred a rush through

Yeqon's body, he sucked in the clean smell of it, tasted the past, present and future.

The softness of his face hardened into coarse angles when the light spluttered into darkness. The portal couldn't maintain its beam for long with the stone circle so badly damaged, so desperately in need of repair. Yeqon's hand blazed with energy as he passed by the last of the fallen sarsen stones. Just like the earth tremor that had toppled it from its pillars, he could so easily elevate it whilst the workers slept, set it back in place and have the portal bringing A'veans in and out before the moon sank.

But no, that would make too much sense, wouldn't it my Father? He spat, the insult to I'el unforgivable, so he did it again.

His fingers slid further across the freezing stones, trembled with temptation, then curled in on themselves. He stared towards the work encampment. Dying fires dotted the landscape where a hundred exhausted men slept. The smell of roasted stag still strong on the air, foxes snuck amongst the camp, dashing about stealing the left overs, their yaps disturbing an otherwise silent pre-dawn.

Yeqon looked back at the sarsen stone, his jaw ached with impatience. If he repaired it, the humans would have no purpose other than eating and fucking… and both of those they did all too well. He chuckled quietly, he couldn't blame them for that though, eating and fucking were his favourite things too... and warring. By the Throne, he missed a good fight. But, left to pleasure alone, humanity would never be forced to think, to learn, to evolve and that would mean he would never be free of the place. He rolled his eyes and made his way back to the edge of the forest, wings sucking away into his spine.

An owl cried, he felt the draught of it tousle his hair as it disappeared deep within the forest, a screaming rat in its claws. Other birds rustled in the trees; their morning song struck the silence from the night. Yeqon leaned back against the same tree trunk and watched the encampment, impatient for the humans to stir, to just get on with it so he could get back to warmer weather and more pleasurable activities. His mind fell back to food and fucking, his smile returned.

Chapter
Four

Dawn slashed a pale light across muddied flats, the frigid morning air finally roused the last of wearied humans. Yeqon unbound his crossed arms, clenched large hands until the knuckles whitened. It had been months of his own company, boredom was evolving into something darker, a slithering bleakness that inhabited the periphery of his mind.

His hands stung, fists unbound and his fingers released. Yeqon's lip curled at the sight of bloody crescents across his palms. Blood pinpricked with the shimmer of A'vean power pooled in the lines until he tipped his hands and let it flow. Each droplet glimmered, crimson drizzled down, splashing red into a fresh dusting of snow. The ground drank it up, dark rivulets clawed across a crisp, icy white that sucked at his bare feet.

Yeqon's brows furrowed, he stamped into the bloody mess, leaving a slushy red puddle behind. His jaw feathered; he sucked in the cold air as he recalled a memory. Satanos, blood reminded him so very much of that ancient, long-gone world. A thriving wilderness with grey-skinned creatures similar to humans, but so very much more evolved and independent of thought. He had liked the inhabitants, helped them to the very best of his ability, yet, in the end they met an unforeseeable demise. The recollection brought a bitterness to the back of his throat and he swallowed hard. It was the reason he was here, on the Earth… Purgatory for a prior mission that didn't see the appropriate outcome.

He resisted the urge to peer up to the heavens again, felt the need to shield his emotions from his creator. This assignment was an overreach of a punishment for Satanos, nothing more, nothing less. Earth was an opportunity for redemption, to do the right thing… what exactly was the right thing? Yeqon's mouth thinned until his lips were a hard, pale line. His head shook slowly.

"Redemption…" He spat again.

Thunder grumbled, Yeqon felt the vibration of it in his chest, tasted the crispness of rain on the air. His attention returned to the circular henge, the humans were back on task, grunting and straining, getting nowhere, just as they had done for so long. The air moved around him with the reverberations of their tools banging, cleaving; the echo of terminal strain unmistakable. He could smell the salt of their exhaustion already.

A light rain began, misting the horizon, imbuing the ground with a slipperiness that saw men fall, tools weigh down and feet sucked into frigid mud. The weather quickly settled into a steady downpour, a hazy veil that further slowed progress.

Yeqon shivered, his skin prickled. The cold was annoying, not threatening, but he tugged at his pants, he didn't like the discomfort of his clothes feeling wet, sticking against his skin. He slipped his shirt off, revealing a wide chest covered in battle scars and silvery symbols that shone with the power that coursed strong under his skin.

He took a moment to release his wings, their glow soft and hot; they warmed the air of the immediate surrounds. He sighed with relief as they stretched wide. Having them tucked away was like an annoying itch unscratched, and he took every opportunity to scratch that itch. Their light, purest of white, cut through the deepening shadows of the forest behind. He cracked his neck, dulled his wings glow, lest an errant human pass by and be blinded, or worse, by their power.

The rain pressed harder, breached the lush canopy, and seared through his wings. The sizzling was loud, enough to expose his position. Yeqon grimaced, yet another reason to loathe this place. He drew the wings back within his body, already cramped, unrelieved, his body coiled too tight and ready to explode. His eyes thinned towards the henge.

The aging stones quickly became awash, mud thickened and he heard the river to the east fill to gushing. The trees around him spoke of the storm's strength. Cracking and groaning, their branches lurched, leaves peppered the air, yellowed and brown, sticking to his skin.

Yeqon's face screwed up as he watched the humans struggle to maintain their footing in the cloggy slop under the weight of a great blue sarsen stone. It was the final one to be put back into place, the last element to reignite the portal to its full power. Rich with a vein of chromious, a seam of enduring and eternal power; it was these very stones that energised the portals across the earth. Yeqon's brow quirked at the thought of that word… power. This henge was the most important on Earth. Theus, one of the Eloi, discovered the power of the bluestones after I'el first sent the Eloi to investigate Earth for signs of sentient life. It was the Eloi who built these portals, this one being the first of many that made transference travel between worlds immensely easier and more expedient for A'veans. Yeqon licked his lips, rubbed the tips of his fingers across his chin, grazing through a thicker stubble. He could almost taste the metallic buzz of leaving this forsaken planet long behind when the portal reignited.

Power…Hmmm.

The appearance of A'vean portals across the world had, of course, enamoured humans of all creeds to the Watchers. At first they were terrified and cowered in their caves, hid in the mud of their swamps. They screamed and squawked at them, flung stones and crudely sharpened sticks at any Watcher they came upon. It only took the accidental incineration of one or two humans for them to stop their feeble resistance.

Once humanity realised A'veans were sharers of knowledge, healers of their ailments, the less than impressive intellect of humanity meant they immediately worshipped Yeqon and his kin as Gods. That in itself wasn't an issue for Yeqon, he often smiled at the thought. However, it was the time they had to retreat into the shadows, whisper in the dreams of men and women, for as they were instructed…

Worshipped you will not be, shadows and dreams are what you shall become. That was the last time he had heard a word from I'el, and those years were now an immeasurable blur in Yeqon's memory.

Anger prickled under Yeqon's skin once more as he recalled his time on Earth. Rage clawed red up his neck. Living in the shadows diminished him, made him feel like a snake slithering unseen, and it made their covert use of the portals more difficult. Occasionally a Watcher was witnessed, glimpsed passing by, or descending from the heavens upon a great light. The worshipping continued. It was out of their hands, so the Watchers allowed humans to believe what they wished, as long as peace and progression of their evolution continued. They just did not share the fact with the suddenly silent I'el.

There was, however, a beauty in their adoration. It meant the humans cared for the portals, maintained them in a pristine manner, repaired them when the bowels of the earth, the weather and time clawed to reclaim the ancient stones.

A breeze gusted past him, its bite yanked Yeqon from his miserable thoughts.

The hairs on his neck stood to attention, he cocked his ear to the left, a smile tugged his lips.

"Still can't sneak up on me, Asbel."

A deep throated chuckle closed in on Yeqon, he felt the breath of it on the back of his neck.

"Not you, friend, but you should see me drop an unsuspecting human," Asbel laughed a little louder. "The way their eyes bulge when I appear from thin air… ah, gets the pulse racing." He laughed again, the deep rumble petering out as he set his eyes upon the henge.

"You're *still* here?"

"Hmph," Yeqon grunted.

"I could repair this in the draw of a breath," Asbel said.

Yeqon's head swivelled slowly, the thought of punching the teeth from Asbel's mouth was appealing. He could make a necklace from them, gift them to I'el when the portal was repaired.

"As could we all, Asbel." Yeqon sucked his own teeth, the image of throttling Asbel faded. His eyes flitted momentarily upwards, that unsatisfied rage made them burn. "But it is not for us to interfere with the humans, as you *well* know."

"It makes no sense, Yeqon. This portal is integral. It's essential. Having it unreliable for so long for the sake of them." He jerked his chin towards the workforce. "It has inhibited our travel for far too long. I wish to visit my family but cannot." Asbel cracked his dark knuckles in the same way that Yeqon did. "We are meant to watch them, not interfere with them, I understand this, but the irony is that our very freedom of movement is limited by that rule." The sweeping curls of light that hugged Asbel's right eye glimmered, the light paled his face, highlighting murky crescents under his eyes.

Yeqon tapped his own dormant mark, his light always subdued, tucked away. Asbel nodded in understanding, the power coursing under his skin faded and the Mark of A'vean dulled around his eye.

"Apologies, by the Throne, my emotions get the better of me," Asbel said.

Yeqon nodded, "I understand, my friend." He clucked his tongue, slapped Asbel on the shoulder. "Indeed, it is beyond comprehension that we suffer at the hands of the ineptitude of a subspecies." Yeqon sniffed sharply, "We must not show ourselves, quiver in the shadows, let humans evolve in their own time. Yet here we are, subject to the whims of nature destroying our portal with incompetence and stupidity the only course of action. It makes my eyes bleed and my soul wither." Yeqon flicked his hand towards the toiling humans.

Asbel and Yeqon stood in companionable silence for a time, arms folded, watching the worksite. The air rose again; the trees rustled.

"Ged'erel," Yeqon greeted him with a sharp nod.

Ged'erel stood a hand taller than both Asbel and Yeqon. Older by an age, his smooth skin, the sharp edges of his face, belied the wisdom and weariness of his existence.

"You're still here, I see. I am surprised you haven't shrivelled up from boredom… or murdered them all." Ged'erel half laughed, half scoffed, his face curling into a snarl when he set sight on the humans.

"It's been many moons, Yeqon," Ged'erel said. Asbel nodded in agreeance.

"Believe me, old friend, I am withered," Yeqon said, pulled a twig from the lurching branches and poked it into the corner of his mouth. His shoulders fell as he chewed the wood, he crossed his arms behind his head, and leaned back into the tree.

"I am well aware of how long I have suffered this posting," Yeqon mumbled, more to himself. "The last stone is close to being raised into position. The very moment it is set, the very second the portal is restored, I will return permanently to the mid-east region where the weather is better, and the women more agreeable." His attention flickered skyward briefly.

You'll not take all my pleasures, dear Father.

Asbel coughed, jolting Yeqon's attention back to the salty odour of the human toil carrying upon the whistle of a burgeoning breeze. He peeled his lips back with disgust and pinched his nose.

"You smell it too?" Asbel asked.

They both sneered, Asbel covered his mouth and nose with his hand and mumbled, "If I'm not required here..."

"Go, there is no point all of us rotting away with boredom. Sort out last meal, I've a hunger upon me." Yeqon pressed the smooth curves of his abdomen, "Make it a feast, invite everyone who is nearby."

Asbel nodded sharply. "And entertainment?" Asbel's attention flickered to the sky, but he lowered his eyes quickly, almost fast enough to appear that he cowered.

"Why not? I'el has long forgotten us," Yeqon answered and slapped Asbel on the shoulder.

Ged'erel sniffed, a brightness shimmered across the blue of his eyes. "I shall bring the company… I know your predilections well enough Yeqon, do I not?" His mouth curled into a smile; a boyish charm blossomed momentarily upon his cheeks before being shrouded by a weariness that aged Ged'erel instantly.

Lust wet Yeqon's mouth, he licked his lips, the same half-smile as Ged'erel, that same set-in darkness of his eyes. "That you do my friend, that you do," Yeqon answered. "Be away with you, if they don't sort this out soon, I'll raze it all and rebuild it myself, no matter the consequence." Yeqon crossed his arms, the muscles tense, his attention unashamedly on the sky. "We will see if I'el really is paying attention."

"Give them the day, they are nearly finished, don't tempt our fate again, please Yeqon. Satanos gave us enough trouble," Asbel said, his attention firmly on the henge, not daring to look up again.

Yeqon's fingers dug into his arms, a tremor barely suppressed, his teeth ground as he inclined his head. "Very well," he said, his pupils dilated so wide the colours of the cosmos were momentarily obliterated before their A'vean spectrum pushed back to the surface.

"Come Asbel, we will see Yeqon before the new moon, I am sure." Ged'erel tapped Asbel, and jerked his head towards the middle of the forest. Ged'erel was already on his way, wings alight, no care for the rules.

"See you at sunset," Asbel said, he followed Ged'erel. The darkness of the forest burned away as they drew their Marks of A'vean to life, and disappeared under the power of their light.

Yeqon stayed a while longer under the tree, recalling a time long ago when he helped the Eloi round up blank eyed humans; accidents of evolution in his opinion. The Eloi dragged them from the swamps well before they were ready, like babes plucked too soon from a womb. I'el had tended humanity with just enough brain matter to urge them away from self-annihilation, but not enough to learn and grow without Yeqon and his brethren whispering from the shadows; persistent mosquitoes in their ears.

Twig chewed to a pulp, it suddenly tasted foul, of dirt and rot. Yeqon spat it out, pulled woody threads from his teeth and wiped the corner of his mouth with the back of his hand. He edged away from the tree, stopped and sniffed the air. The temperature had dropped appreciably. He breathed deeply, smelled that mineral note that warned of worse weather.

The pace of the construction intensified when thunder called in the distance; the workers low, repetitive work chant kicked up a notch. They understood the weather's warning too. Lightning urged the humans along as conditions deteriorated rapidly. The leader group, five men with prominent brows and large hands, yelled in their throaty language, pointing animatedly at the final great stone they had hoisted upon a scaffold. It swayed pendulously, waiting to be lowered into place. The storm grew, winds whipped at the beams of the scaffold. It creaked; humans shouted warnings. Yeqon straightened, jaw clenched, heart pacing just a little faster, his tongue swept over his lips.

Mud-caked workers now screamed in panic, pointing to the stone. Some rushed beneath the precariously swaying monolith, some pushed extra supports against the scaffold; others fell to their knees in prayer.

"No one's listening," Yeqon mumbled towards those with hands clasped. He huffed. "If I'el won't talk to me, he isn't going to listen to you lot." The prayer group dissipated, a tall bald man with a streak of black tar down the middle of his face reached for a worker who had been pointlessly leaning upon a shovelling tool. The worker yelped as he was pulled aside, dragged into the middle of the henge and pinned down, one worshipper upon each limb. The man screamed, begged, even from where he stood, Yeqon saw the stain of bodily waist darken his clothing. Yeqon shook his head as a length of dull steel glinted when the portal light flashed momentarily. The knife arced downward towards the victim bent over the altar stone. A guttural cry echoed the circle of the henge, had other workers stop, their bodies rigid with wonder… probably more so with terror.

The victim's body went flaccid, blood was strong on the air as the man with the tar streak sawed up and down.

"I didn't teach you that," Yeqon muttered as he watched the sacrifice's chest open. His heart was removed, yanked with a quick tug, and held aloft as lightning flashed across the sky. More monotone prayers were called to the heavens… heavens that were deaf to their pleas.

Yeqon grimaced. "Fools."

No God intervened, there wasn't one to listen, but of course, he couldn't tell humanity that, he was forbidden to share such important knowledge. I'el was long ago distracted by other worlds, by more exciting adventures.

The reward for the blood just spilled was the hand of the wind clutching more forcefully at the great sarsen stone, lurching it even further. The feet of the scaffolding sunk on one side, the softening ground quickly giving in to the weather. The humans yelled; their muscles strained under the weight of the pendulous stone as they desperately attempted to raise it up to complete the outer circle of the henge.

Yeqon's mouth wet as screams chorused beneath a closer rumble of thunder, his hands clenched repetitively. He ached to barge straight over, smack them all more stupid than they already were and fix the damned portal. But as his toes wriggled, as his body itched to move, another man screamed as he was dragged from the work line into the centre of the henge. Held down just like the other, the still blood-slicked knife swept down once more, his throat opened under the kiss of steel. The sacrifice's body twitched and jerked, and this time the smell of shit mingled with the hot thickness of blood. Nearby workers vomited as crimson ribbons slicked into the air, disappearing upon each gust of wind; the last pumps of a dying heart sprayed red across his murderers. Still no God, still no reprieve. Yeqon shook his head again, and snorted; it was almost amusing now.

He eyed the sky, arched a brow. "Still no interest? They kill themselves for you. Is that really what you want?" No answer, as usual. Yeqon spat and watched on. The hesitation in the workers was palpable, he could smell the tang of their fear as that same group of worshippers huddled around the altar stone, perhaps considering a third sacrifice. A handful of workers dashed toward the forest; tools thrown aside. Yeqon sunk behind a tree as they ran past, ignorant of a power more terrifying than those they were fleeing. Once they had been swallowed into the forest, he rounded out of the shadows and thinned his eyes towards the henge, waiting the next move, knowing more death was on its way.

Freezing gusts pushed against him. The workers struggled against its force. The storm's biting breath made Yeqon shiver a little, so he released a wedge of wing light from his spinal column, let that heat lick across his skin. The weather's building wrath was now overcoming the humans. They coughed and shivered, and it now tugged the stone heavily to the left. The bluestone's movement built momentum, it swayed faster upon its thick ropes. Hail thundered down, crashing against the henge, an ominous high-pitched tune echoed within the great circle. The humans struggled in the sticky, muddy slush, their movements slow and laboured. One simply collapsed, his skin turned blue, then yellow, then the pasty white of death.

Yeqon heard the gathering around the altar stone intensify their prayers, a throaty, melodic chant. In any other situation he might quite enjoy the sound of it, the in-tune harmony, but this day it was pointless and laughable.

"Save your breath," he mumbled.

The ropes netting the swinging stone began to fray. Yeqon's sharp senses heard the first snaps of twine, he saw the whiskers of it flare wide and spin undone. The hail passed; the wind settled as though perhaps nature felt pity. An eerier quiet set upon the landscape as a dull sun cleaved momentarily through a sliver in the brackish clouds. It glinted off the rain, a sickly yellow glow, obliterated as thunderclouds coalesced into a blackening plume. The day darkened into a dusky hue. No, nature did not care.

The men toiled on, their skin flushed and rain-slicked, their breaths white plumes of panic. The rope whined and twirled almost completely undone. Its flaxen threads seared away, Yeqon smelled the roasted burn of it slice across a hundred calloused palms. The scaffolding cracked again, one leg of it bowed. It lurched further to the left, pulled by the stone. The feet of it quickly sunk, its other leg bowed, the cross beams snapped. The great blue sarsen stone flipped, it swung vertically from a single length of rope. The workers stepped up into a heightened state of panic, dashing about pointlessly, uselessly reaching for tools with absolutely no capacity to stop what was about to happen.

The Mark of A'vean that spiralled the skin of Yeqon's right eye tingled and he let it burn to the surface, illuminating the dark clutch of forested shadows he still hid within. The power within him grew, it urged to be released. His back itched, his wings ached to be free. He took a step forward, then another. Yeqon kept walking until he breached the tree line of the forest. His light shone brighter, a shadow cast long behind him. A darkness underpinned his eyes, his lips felt too dry, his mortal heart tapped uncomfortably fast against his ribs. A quick glance upwards, "Still nothing? Well, I'm done with your ignorance, your rules. Look at what you have done!" Yeqon cracked his knuckles, let his wings out a little further as I'el continued with his silence.

There was a loud groan, the sound of more wood splitting, that giant stone swung lower by the second. Yeqon stepped out further again, any of them could see him now if they looked back, if they weren't so enamoured by the unfolding tragedy about to happen. He let his light shine a little brighter, feeling emboldened by the decision he had committed to.

Desperate screams of terror were drowned out by the song of the storm. Unheard, blood spilled, with no help from their God, the humans gave in. Their fingers unbound and they let the last of the ropes go. The ground rumbled with retreating feet, prayers quickly forgotten, commitment to the portal and the Watchers superseded by the instinctual craving for life.

The great stone lintel lurched one last time. Legs heavy with mud, bodies exhausted, the humans, no matter their efforts, moved too slowly, sucked down, tangling amongst themselves in panic. As the ropes slid free, snapping, flicking, giving in under the weight of the stone, the scaffolding collapsed with no further warning. Lightning sliced across the sky; thunder cracked through a stunned silence.

Yeqon released his wings fully, he rose with the next gust and pushed forwards, his pupils dilated into wide, black discs. He moved slowly, waiting; watching the carnage unfold as the great blue stone fell.

Chapter

Five

A dull thud brought everyone to a state of paralysed disbelief. All movement ceased. The humans turned, mouths agape, eyes wide, staring at the foot of the henge. Yeqon hid high above the portal, his luminous power camouflaged within the lightning and the grey and white of the storm that enveloped him. He squinted, trying to discern the humans amongst the mud they clawed through. The bluestone that had moments ago swung overhead, now sat snug, deeply entrenched in the ground, the scaffolding and rope collapsed around it. There were no more screams, just a shocked silence. The workers and worshipers alike stared at bloodied body parts protruding from beneath the stone. The wind blew at their stillness, tugged at the deer skins and linens that uselessly hugged frost-bitten skin. Understanding released the silence when a guttural cry cut through the howl of the storm. The humans surged towards their fallen.

Yeqon stayed hidden within nature's temper, doing what he did best… watching. His hands rolled over and over, he lowered a little so as to see a little more, his wings now beat in time with the errant bursts of portal light. A thickening bloodied pool filled the depression around the fallen stone. Hungry mud slurped it up, only to be refilled twice more before the blood coagulated, its source flow stilled. The smell of death ripened the air, Yeqon's nostrils flared. He lowered a little further to sharpen the image below, the risk of his discovery now almost void since his mind was decided, since I'el showed no care at all.

Two hands poked out from under the stone, fingers corpse-white and contorted in strange angles. A foot and a half torso jerked a moment or two under a corner of stone, before stilling into a permanent rest. A new silence filled the air, the rain even eased as though the storm also felt the tragedy.

After a time, that even to Yeqon felt like hours, the humans awoke to the catastrophe and a chaotic rescue effort followed. Uselessly, they used hand and pick, sticks and stones. They sheared away pieces of rock to dig for the remnants of their fallen. It was impossible, they were too feeble of body and mind to do anything of use. They hollered more prayers to the sky, looking up for help, for hope. Their eyes searched past Yeqon, their ignorance, their one-sightedness looked straight through him. Prayers unanswered, many ran for the forest. The sharp crack of branches preceded logs being dragged back to wedge under the stone.

Yeqon cocked his head, an eyebrow peaked. They were learning. The corner of his mouth lifted slightly, he nodded, almost unwilling to acknowledge his approval. He moved closer again and watched quietly as they struggled to find purchase in the ground, the logs heavy and cumbersome. The wind carried their cries as they grunted in unison to leverage the stone away from the bodies.

Thunder cracked, clouds converged a darker shade of grey, an ominous witness to the carnage. Rain returned, hardening into a biting pelt; its empathy gone. An impossible sludge developed; water immediately filled the holes they dug. The remaining workers began backing away, peering skyward again, sight blinded by the driving rain; fear and defeat drained the colour from them. They were abandoning the rescue, leaving the henge repairs; too scared, too incapable.

The portal beam stuttered; its light too unstable, its power too muted to be predictably useful. Yeqon's patience waned, his teeth ground. He looked skyward; arms outstretched. "Now is the time to save your precious playthings. Any objections to this madness?" His mouth peeled back into an easy sneer.

"Your message is received, Father. *I* am to take charge of this chaos." Yeqon spat into the roiling clouds, imagining the more exciting things he could be doing on a thousand other planets.

"By the Throne, be damned with it!" He flexed his shoulders, ignited his wings of light brighter than he had ever dared in the presence of humans. They spanned him two lengths, he rolled his head, the relief made him shudder. He lowered towards the henge. Rain sheared across his skin, searing into hot steam as it hit the heat of his wings.

Yeqon's shadow succumbed to the sickly green daylight as the sun completely retreated. He circled around the verge of the forest towards the clearing where the portal stood in near completeness. The light of his wings atop the bleakness of the landscape became a beacon that drew the attention of the men far below. Eyes widened, their terror at the sight of him weakened their legs, garbled their tongues. The retreating humans sunk to the ground, incapacitated by the sight of a Watcher. Hands fisted in front of their faces, none dared to look up.

Lightning struck the far-off hills that hugged a bare landscape to the north, to the south the storm blew in faster from across the ocean. Yeqon peered into the murky horizon, with a determination to complete his tasks here and promptly return to the mid-east deserts. His patience had dried up like a desiccating corpse. Everything was at least tolerable there. It was warm, dry and the company abundant and willing in all things pleasurable that this planet could offer. He drew a breath and returned his gaze to the swarm of incompetence below.

The iridescence of his wings flared across the pallor of the northern humans. They cowered ever lower, faces pressed into the mud, their filthy bodies blending into the deep grey of the henge. Yeqon grunted in their direction, didn't tone down his power as he knew he should. He couldn't be bothered. There were so many of them, they'd breed more if a few were lost this day.

A group of smooth-faced youths, knowing no better, peered up in wonder as Yeqon hovered overhead, deciding how he might intervene. In an instant they screamed, grabbed for their eyes and rolled through the mud in tight balls, their bodies twitched and fitted. Blood oozed between their fingers; their breaths desperate grunts. Elders crawled to them, pulling strips from their robes and wrapped their blinded eyes from the light of a Watcher Angel... from the light of Yeqon.

The elders clawed at trinkets that jingled around their necks, holy objects they revered, and garbled commands to the wounded who howled in their pain. Blood-soaked rags didn't quiet the agony of their scorched eyes.

Yeqon could have, he should have dulled his energy after that moment, yet that corner of his mouth quirked up once more and his mouth watered the way it always did before battle.

Why should I care? he thought.

His hands clenched tight; the muscles of his forearms corded with pent up frustration. He wondered how different this world might be if he could wield his power the way he had elsewhere? Such easy pickings on Earth, simple beings, but no, I'el for whatever His grand plan was, insisted upon the most ludicrous ideology that humans evolve with as little intervention as possible.

Devolve more like it.

Yeqon's eyes darkened, his nostrils flared. He shifted his wings, the humans gasped under the light and bowed impossibly lower. He waited for them to still, to stop their snivelling... to show some sense of self-respect.

Only once the squelching of their bodies slipping in the mud was all that cut through the whistle of the wind, did Yeqon descend to the ground. He grimaced as his feet sunk into bloody puddles skirting the fallen stone. He felt another buzz in the air, his skin prickled and he peered over his shoulder towards the forest. He was alone for now, but someone was on their way.

"Move!" Yeqon snapped. The humans shuffled away, praying their useless prayers as they obeyed him. He smiled as they fell over themselves. Subservience was one of the few pleasures on this world, and he milked it wherever he could, when the others weren't watching to keep him in check. He peered over his shoulder again, the buzz in the atmosphere was getting stronger.

Yeqon stepped slowly around the stone, he grimaced at the body parts sticking out from underneath it. Something in the gore caught his eye. He squatted down, angled his right wing so its light shone brighter at the base of the stone. His smile returned; his tongue swept across his bottom lip. Swirling in bloodied water that pooled in thin trenches… was a human soul. Its misty length coiled in on itself, then it unwound slowly and poked about its watery confines. Its movement became more erratic, as though it was confused, not knowing where it was or where to go. Yeqon's brow quirked, he cocked his head. He ran thumb and forefinger across his chin, his calloused fingers like gravel against his skin. An idea formed in his mind as the soul weaved through the clawed fingers of one of the dead.

Yeqon caught someone watching him. He hissed at the man, who slapped his face back into the ground. Whilst all eyes were averted, he reached out and wriggled his fingers at the soul.

"Come," he said as softly as he was capable. It pulled away and sunk back within the water, its soft glow a moon within the puddle. He called it again in his thoughts, a gentler song to his words. *I give you release.* The soul hesitantly poked back out, rippled the puddle and tasted the air.

"Come to me," Yeqon coaxed, and the soul eased from the water. It snaked along the ground until it pooled, a tiny fog, at Yeqon's feet. He reached down before anyone saw, snatched it up and slid the soul into a pocket hanging by the hilt of his sword. It writhed in panic against his leg, Yeqon snorted, "You will be the first."

Something dark stirred within Yeqon, his mortal skin tingled pleasurably, his heart beat with an excitement that fanned that darkness. His Mark of A'vean burned a little hotter across his face and he groaned, relishing the pain of it. He thought back to Satanos, recalled the power he had wielded over its inhabitants. The pulse in his neck thundered harder.

A spray of hail tore Yeqon away from indulgent thoughts. He took a step back from the monolithic stone, away from the stinking entrails paling underneath it. The portal stuttered behind him, its beam into the heavens remained patchy, and he knew it was now up to him to repair it. He moved away from the still cowering humans, curled his lips at the sight of them, before focusing again upon the fallen stone. Already, even with the scent of death muted by the weather, ravens circled overhead for a meal. A few landed on the east side of the henge, a large bold one fluttered within a few feet of Yeqon, unaffected by who and what he was.

He let the ravens indulge themselves on whatever they could scavenge, the humans cried louder upon hearing hungry squawks as the birds tore flesh from finger and toe. Yeqon rolled his eyes, dulled his light and elevated a little into the air.

"Get up!" he commanded, no lie of kindness in his voice. The humans immediately obeyed, scuttling further back from the henge and pulling themselves to their feet. Yeqon's face glimmered, white hot energy raced down his arms, lighting the veins of his hands. He aimed his palms towards the fallen stone. The boldest of humans gasped with wonder and more were struck blind; writhing bloodied bundles in the mud. The more pious jangled their charms and chanted rhythmically.

"Watch at your peril," Yeqon warned the rest as power erupted within him. His hands shimmered; luminous rivers of light pulsed from palm to fingertip. Snapping bursts of energy sliced through the air. It exploded upon the fallen stone. It wrapped around the width of it, coating the sarsen until the rock shifted in the mud. The mud clung to it, slurped for its prize, but Yeqon's power sucked it up with a loud pop, bone and flesh glued to its underside.

The pious chanted with increasing fervour as Yeqon raised his palms and the great stone lifted in silence, as light as a feather. He grimaced as he coaxed it into position, gently jolting it until the human remains peeled away and fell into the hole left in its wake. Pulling, then pushing in just the right measure, he guided it up, over his head, past the chanting ones and nestled it atop the last two pillars with a dull thud. Yeqon's hands dulled, he sighed, wiped sweat from his brow. He nodded in satisfaction and relief; the circle of the henge was repaired.

"Step away!" he yelled at the prayerful and the just plain stupid who still hung too close for their own good.

The portal shimmered; its light brightened. The ground shuddered; a great cord plucked within the bones of the earth and a thick beam of whiteness soared towards the heavens. The humans swayed; hands clasped, they prayed anew. Yeqon rolled his eyes.

"Clean them up!" Yeqon pointed towards what was left of the bodies. All but one with souls attached, still unaware that they were dead, still probing the slick ground in ignorance of their fate. Yeqon's throat bobbed, he swallowed hard, not really understanding why he cared what the humans saw now. But when he turned from their attention, one hand slipped to his pocket and felt the wriggle of the first soul, lost and frantic and confused. His lips curled up as a plan formed in the distance of his mind.

The pious continued chanting their prayers as though Yeqon were some form of deity. Their reverberating song grated on his nerves, but he indulged them a moment. As their song intensified, his teeth ground for a very different reason. Each gust of wind brought that familiar buzz closer, a skin plucking feeling that he wouldn't be alone for long. His fingers clawed into fists again, his chest tightened with frustration. He dialled his power down further after another human fell to the ground, blinded. He hastily withdrew his wings of light back within his spine as he admired the now restored, pulsing portal henge.

It hummed softly, warming the immediate surrounds, a faint change in its pitch hinted that someone was incoming. He looked back towards the forest to see the source of the other buzzing, the feeling that made him want to hide the soul, and suppress the power he should not have born in front of humans. He sneered again and wanted to spit, but that insult was saved especially for I'el.

Her light appeared, haloing the tree line, and Yeqon's nails sliced into his palms.

Be damned! His teeth squeaked as he forced a gentler expression, urged his cheeks to pull the fakest of smiles.

"Rise." He ushered the humans up quickly with a flick of his hands, ever aware she had been watching him from the ether, she had seen him step far out of line.

"Bring your wounded here," Yeqon demanded. The humans were guided by their leaders, slipping and stumbling towards Yeqon until they found their footing at his feet. Their eyes bulged; their chests heaved… they were terrified.

"Come closer, you are safe." *For now*, he thought, enjoying their fear, lapping at the taste of it. *She* couldn't sense that, so he breathed in the tang of it as he laid a hand across each one of the men. A pulse of light flashed beneath his palm, each man gasped and fell back, caught by another, bleeding abated, fractures healed.

Yeqon urged the blinded forwards and repeated the gesture.

"You may no longer see, but your pain is now forever relieved and your inner eye opened."

The men blinked, their eyes milky, lids swollen. They probed their eyes with dirty, stubby fingers, tears streaming, tinted red as old blood washed away. They bowed in thanks, wailed and prayed, pulled away by the leaders only for another to pushed towards Yeqon for healing.

Yeqon's attention slid repetitively towards the forest, her arms were crossed, her eyes narrow. His knuckles whitened and his teeth ached in their sockets. He drew a deep breath, looked back to the humans, imagined his most sympathetic voice and played the part expected of him.

"The loss of your companions will be richly rewarded with the arrival of new servants of I'el, the creator of all things." Yeqon's voice reverberated around the henge, he fanned his arms wide, looked up to the sky; the overdone display enamoured his audience all the more. They moaned in awe, looked to the heavens as well, and hailed that which they did not understand.

Yeqon suppressed the urge to roll his eyes. "This restored heavenly gateway is a gift to help you prosper and realise continued peace. Keep it secure, in good order, and revere those who descend to watch over you." He released his wings, fanned them for dramatic effect, lighting himself up just a little to dazzle them all the more. In his mind it sounded more like, *'blah, blah blah.'*

He peered across the horizon again, she was still at the tree line, still watching him, still silent.

You'll not judge me, Kiraal. You're no better than any of us and you know it.

Yeqon's inner dialogue was interrupted by a vibration underfoot. A familiar, rich hum laced the air. The chord of the portal had been struck. It teased the hairs on his arms to attention. Its light flickered a little brighter, its beam penetrated the storm, cleaving through the clouds and up into the heavens. Rain continued, but within the henge, the air was now dry and temperate, reminding Yeqon again of the middle eastern lands he preferred.

"Back away now. The portal is active. You are not safe this close. Your work is done for now. Go home," Yeqon commanded and pointed to the carnage in the depression where the great bluestone had fallen. "Take your dead with you."

The humans bowed, finished their ridiculous prayers and immediately obeyed. The elders pointed here and there, and a handful of men dragged body parts quickly away, ravens in pursuit, cawing at their meal disturbed. Yeqon grimaced discreetly as he watched them melt back into the forest, back to their primitive villages, back to the ignorance that drove him wild with frustration. Not one of them noticed the presence of Kiraal. She played the game as he was supposed to, she did as I'el commanded so utterly perfectly, and it made him want to peel out of his skin.

Once the humans were gone, Kiraal flew from the tree line, her gentle light bathed the landscape. She settled next to Yeqon, flicked a braid behind her shoulder and crossed her arms, a parcel of clothing tucked under them.

"Kiraal." He inclined his head and reached for her. They clasped each other's forearm in greeting. Kiraal smiled, leaned into him, touched her richly lit Mark of A'vean to his, a K'ufili, a kiss, a mark of respect between Watchers.

"So formal Yeqon. Since when have you called me anything other than Kira? Is someone important watching?" She smiled richly, but her eyes remained a steely shade, one hand hovered above a great sword that hung from her hip. "It has been some time since we have met, but please, we need no such formality and you know it." Kira's smile faded; the swirl of her rainbow tinted eyes intensified. "Are you well? Does something trouble you?"

Am I well? The question was like a poker to his frustration. It stirred a fire that he struggled to contain.

"Troubled? Of course not. I am well, Kira. And you?"

By the love of I'el this mindless banter could sear my soul from this body. One could only hope.

He held a hand out to guide her towards the portal as its beam flickered and hissed with the imminent arrival.

"Expecting someone?" Yeqon asked.

Kira nodded; her eyes sparkled brighter as they stood a few feet from the altar stone. He noticed her stare at the fresh bloodstains, but she said nothing.

"A clue?" he asked, but before she could answered, the portal beam shimmered, its power thrummed underfoot. The ground quaked, the echo of it set birds a flight within the forest, a smudge of black flocking left and right until they sunk back into the safety of the canopy.

The light flashed, the whiteness of it deepened until it was opaque with power. The mud surrounding the henge thickened, its moisture sucked from the ground until it was left hard and cracked. The great sarsen stones spoke, an ancient song circled within the henge, echoing the intensity of its power. Veins of moss and lichen fluoresced across the grey face of the stones, a bioluminescent verdigris that pulsed in tune with the portal, each stone the face of a galaxy, each sarsen a guide, a map powered by the elements.

Yeqon's attention drew to a shape descending within the portal. Whiter than white, an A'vean soul in its true, majestic form. Sleek, their wings undulated slowly as they settled upon the altar stone. Their shape shivered and stretched, coalescing into a solid, mortal form. The henge shuddered once before its energy dulled and the light faded to a faint regular pulse.

The hairs of Yeqon's neck rose and a growl rumbled deep in his chest. His shoulders sunk ever so slightly.

Kira ran to the altar, arms wide, wings brighter than before. The A'vean soul turned their head towards her. She finished shaking herself into naked form as Kira approached, smoothing out the clothing she held.

"Ugh… anyone else," Yeqon muttered to himself, his eyes followed the portal beam straight up. "You do this deliberately, of that I am quite sure," Yeqon spoke to the ever-silent I'el.

The new arrival stepped from the altar stone, as tall as any other Watcher with swirling rainbow-coloured eyes and the tell-tale white hair, bleached from the A'vean power coursing beneath her skin. Her Mark of A'vean flashed as Kira approached and Kea smiled widely.

"Kea!" Kira exclaimed, they hugged briefly before Kira passed Kea the clothes, helping her slip on the pants and a shirt altered to accommodate wings. "The weather here, its unpredictable and the humans… well they are strangely offended by nakedness," Kira giggled.

Kea ran her hands down the stiff fabric, rubbed it between thumb and forefinger, nodded, then frowned. "Rather strange." She readjusted the top, rolled the cuffs of the pants up from her ankles and set her weapons snuggly back in place around her hips. "Better."

Kira patiently waited for Kea's comfort to be tended; hands clasped over her heart. Kea looked up, smiled broadly, stepped forwards. "Dearest Kiraal." They embraced, held together with an enduring K'ufili that made Yeqon want to rip Kira's wings from her spine.

Kea stepped back, held Kira's face in her hands, her jaw clenched as though holding back the emotion so clearly shining across her eyes. She assessed Kira with great concern etched across her face. "You are well?"

"I'm fine, everything is fine." Kira's hands ran affectionately up and down Kea's arms, they pressed their marks together once more, lighting the space around them a little brighter. Kea pulled away again, made no attempt to hide the fact she'd noticed Yeqon watching, then pulled Kira's lips to her own.

Yeqon rolled his eyes, ran his tongue inside his lips, picked his nails, rolled his eyes again.

When Kea and Kira separated, Kea took Kira's hand and led her away from the altar stone, her other hand resting upon her own sword, a twin of Kira's. They threaded through the henge stones and halted a few feet from Yeqon, a coy smile played upon Kea's mouth.

"Still an emotionless black hole, Yeqon?" Kea unlaced her fingers from Kira and reached for Yeqon. Their arms clasped and they shared a greeting; their K'ufili brief. Yeqon pulled sharply away once the formality was tended.

"Emotions, Kea, serve no purpose other than to distract from our mission," Yeqon bowed his head. "As pointless as it may be."

Kea's eyes scanned Yeqon, he could feel her judgement and a snarl tempted the edge of his mouth, but he swallowed it away.

"You're disappointed to see me, Yeqon?" Kea asked, brows arched, hand hovering near her weapons belt again.

"You've moved on," he snorted. "I'm neither pleased nor disappointed. I am merely… present." His eyes flickered to her hand, then back to the cool of her appraising gaze.

Kea huffed; a more genuine smile drew a dewy blush to the new flesh of her cheeks.

"Well, that somewhat bare-faced insult aside, you made it perfectly clear a long time ago that it was lust, not love that we shared. Am I to never love again? Am I to pine for your attention eternally?" Her mouth quirked, the challenge thrown down.

They stared unashamedly at each other, Yeqon unable to hide his attention lingering on Kea's new and finely toned human body. She looked every bit a formidable warrior in this new skin, just as she always had. Now though, he understood the unique senses of human flesh, the soft and tender places that could and would bring even the most hardened warrior to their knees. Kea had done this for him in the past in A'vean form, imagine what….

He resisted the warmth pooling under his skin, grit his teeth, and held his tongue lest he give away the shake of his resolve at the sight of her.

Kea held Yeqon's suddenly glassy gaze. She deliberately and slowly took in the rich expanse of his mortal form. It was all new, unusual, and Yeqon could see in the way she pressed her mouth tight, that she too was caught off guard. The blush of Kea's skin deepened, its tendrils crawled up her neck. She rubbed at the unusual newness of the body she wore. Kea chuckled, shook her head and took a step back, Yeqon smiled, battle won.

Kira reached for Kea's hand and sidled close.

"I'm sure you would have preferred anyone else to portal in?" Kea asked, amusement lit her voice as she hugged Kira close.

"Well, we can't always have what we want now, can we Kea?" Yeqon widened his arms, circled slowly, showcasing the henge. "We are but I'el's humble servants, are we not? Our desires are at the whim of our benevolent creator, are they not?"

"I am grateful for all that I'el, bless His presence, provides me." Kea stretched out her new body again, the joints cracking and settling into place. "He has created something most interesting here." She nodded to herself and ran her fingers along the soft texture of her abdomen. "Hmph." Her nails raked though her hair, rubbed it between her fingers then flicked it away. Kea closed her eyes and breathed in, "Smells much better here than other places at least, and I don't mind this at all." She prodded her cheeks, ran her tongue across her lips. "So very delicate, rather sensitive. I think I might come to like this form immensely." Kea smiled, and Kira hugged tighter into her side.

"You will dearest. It can be challenging, but it is the most pleasant of all the worlds I've so far come upon," Kira said.

Yeqon puffed out a breath and walked to the outer circle of the henge.

"Well, if you require nothing else, I've a feast to attend." He released his wings to their widest and brightest as he left the powerful hum of the henge. He fought the urge to peer back at Kea as something unwelcome twinged in his chest. The wind gusted, carrying upon it the whiff of body odour, immediately capturing his attention. His eyes slid to the tree line where he spied a hundred faces staring from the shadows of the forest. Annoyance rumbled deep in Yeqon's chest, he shook his head, thoughts of fleeing to another universe wracked him until his head ached. He turned back to the portal, its addictive glow, and the smell of human excrement had a sweat break across his forehead. Attention caught between the portal, the forest and the decadence of the awaiting feast had his mind cluttered. Not to mention the annoying confusion Kea's appearance stirred in him. His teeth ground, his knuckles cracked.

He turned away again, ready to leave. A handful of humans wanting a better seat at the show were stupid enough to step from the safety of the forest. They fell to the ground immediately, the power of his light simply too much. Yeqon huffed. "Fools." Human curiosity would be their destruction, his desires could well be his own to pursue again one day, so he secretly yearned for humanity to just hurry up and die out.

Yeqon didn't see a future for them or himself on this planet, well, not anything other than a war born of desire and boredom. The thought of bloodshed relaxed the ache in his jaw and the tightness of his scalp. It lifted his spirits in spite of Kea's presence looming closer behind him.

"You're following me, Kea?" Yeqon grumbled as he left the halo of the portal behind.

"*We* are following you, Yeqon. I've been sent to escort you back to the mid-east. You have taken too long to guide this portal back to working order…"

Yeqon spun around. "*I*…" He poked his chest angrily. "*I* have taken too long? Do you actually know the rules of this place? You're only here now to berate me because I had to disregard the directive and repair it just this morning. These humans are imbecilic, Kea!"

His chest heaved, his mark glimmered, his fingers flexed and hovered all too close to his weapons.

Kea put her hands up in defence. "Calm down. I understand, I am but the messenger."

"Calm down, she says." He looked to the sky and spat at it.

"Yeqon, you're angry and frustrated. I see that. We can deal with the details, the issues with the directive later, alright?" Kea pleaded.

"Everyone understands the difficulty of this place Yeqon, your intervention today is not at all unreasonable. Please listen to Kea and let's move through one issue at a time," Kira said, her voice soft, appeasing.

Yeqon's hands relaxed. "Well, what else is it that I'm so abysmally failing?"

Kea sighed, "Don't be so dramatic."

"Five minutes and you call me dramatic? I've lived a hundred thousand human life times here, and you call me dramatic?" His mouth curled up; anger bloomed across his chest.

"Fine, apologies. I acknowledge this has been challenging. I am truly sorry you have not been allowed to see A'vean for so long." Kea's expression saddened; she bowed her head. "It is an unreasonably extended punishment."

Yeqon dulled his power, bowed his head in acknowledgment. "One only wishes to be heard on such matters." He waved impatiently at her. "What else then, hurry up."

"Your extended absence in the mid-east has left the humans settlements to fall apart, quite literally. Apparently, a number of their villages have formed warring factions over resources. I have been tasked with trying to settle it before they annihilate themselves. There are precious few humans in that region as it is, so I'm told." Kea inclined her head respectfully, "With your guidance and expertise, of course I am quite sure we can rectify things quickly."

Yeqon rolled his shoulders back, felt the sting of the unspoken accusation.

"I have been otherwise engaged, watching this lot." Yeqon flung his arm back, indicating the forest. The undergrowth rustled with the still-present humans watching them, the newly blinded still being dragged back within its shelter.

"Indeed, but these ones do not war at present. Their survival is not as under threat. I could just as easily have waited for the portal to be repaired whilst you tended other more pressing matters." Kea eyed the forest one final time. "Well, they aren't under threat from factional fighting, at least." Her brows quirked, her mouth pursed and she turned to Kira.

"Is that how you assess the situation? It is the message I received," Kea asked.

Kira nodded. "This region is secure at present, not progressive, but at least not warring. The mid-east has more stress on the resources, the weather is harsh. Its sands and heat affect the land substantially, but they persist in settling there, despite us gently trying to nudge them along to more productive land." Kira looked at Yeqon. "I did tell you we shouldn't leave them unattended, Yeqon."

Yeqon's hand slid to his sword, his fingers wrapped and unwrapped around the handle. "They aren't alone, Kira. Watchers are present."

"Yes, but you are in charge, and it is to you they look up to," Kira answered.

Kea edged in front of Kira as Yeqon smiled, and nodded slowly.

"Yes, Kira you did mention the mid-east, what, fifty moons ago? I should have listened to your sage advice then and left this portal to completely fall apart." His hand slid from the weapon and he inclined his head, "So, to appease all but myself, my feast will have to wait." He turned away and did not look back this time.

Fools, he thought and rose higher into the air. One languid flap and he was miles above the landscape, Kira and Kea close behind.

They flew in uncomfortable silence until Yeqon could hold his tongue no further.

"Why does our beloved Father leave them to hit the lowest level before he allows us to intervene? I could have settled such feuds with a wave of my hand, Kea, and you well know it.

Does he enjoy their suffering? Does he enjoy mine at having to nearly fade away from the boredom of it all?" Yeqon banked hard left, evading a flock of gulls.

Kira coasted in by his side. "It's not for us to question," she said.

Kea nodded, "Kira is correct, Yeqon, we do as we are ordered, that is all, we are warriors, it is our directive. I'el commands that we bring an end to this conflict now, so we shall."

Yeqon sped up, rage rumbled in his chest.

"I'm thrilled He deigns to speak to you. Do you think I've not begged Him to hear the troubles of the Earth? I've tried, believe me Kea, I have called endlessly for I'el. We could have taught them all they needed from the first breath they drew, prevented the need for all of this. But no, He has ignored my pleas. So yes, let's descend into the bloody feuds of humans now when its most likely too late." Yeqon pushed through a particularly abundant cloud. Rain pelted through his wings until he breached the touch of the storm. He pulled up, hovering in a slick of sunlight, Kea and Kira by his side.

"Ah." Yeqon sighed and wrapped his wings about himself. He shuddered as their light dried his body. "But I'll happily get out of this forsaken weather, *that* is the only reason I'll give them another day of my time." He glanced across the expanse of cloud below, black with endless storms. "Miserable damned planet."

Kea's brows arched, she shivered. "It's not so pleasant, is it?" Her wings deepened, she wrapped their light around herself, copying Yeqon, shielding her new form from the cold. She smiled at the relief.

Kira followed suit, her wings slipping neatly around her body. "It isn't always like this. Some places are really quite lovely."

"I'm hopeful to see them. I've experienced much worse, than this though, I think I'll manage." Kea shook, her wings unwound, her body warm and dry. "Wait until you visit Nautanos, Kira. All water and ice. A very challenging place, but it does have some rather lovely wildlife," Kea said. She smiled, gently tugging Kira's hand as they lifted into a thick ray of sunlight before settling upon an updraft alongside Yeqon.

"Show us the way Yeqon." Kea reached her other hand out. Yeqon pressed his lips tight and touched one finger onto Kea's to establish a connection for transference.

"This will feel like a pull in your belly," Kira glanced at Kea's stomach. "It doesn't hurt, lasts just a moment."

Kea nodded; a hand absently pressed against the curve of her belly in preparation.

"Ready?" Yeqon's voice was low, bitterness sharpened his words and he pulled away from her touch as soon as he could. Kea was the only lover to ever reject him and it sliced through his ego as painfully as any sword through flesh. The urge to just leave them there alone was immense, but he suppressed it, closed his eyes and brought the hills of Babylonia into his thoughts.

Chapter
Seven

The smell hit them first, before their feet touched the ground. Circling birds drew their attention towards the smooth dip of a valley. Kea smothered her face with her hand.

"By the love of I'el!" she gasped.

"Oh no," Kira's fingers laced back through Kea's. "We're too late."

"We are *always* too late with these creatures," Yeqon walked to the rise of the olive orchard they had landed in. He pushed a branch aside, plucked an olive from it and rolled the fruit between his fingers. He surveyed the charred remains of a village. His tongue probed inside his cheek, then swept across his teeth before biting into the unripe fruit. He grimaced, it was bitter, but he rolled it across his tongue anyway. His head shook slowly, spat the pip out and turned around to Kea and Kira.

"There is no love from I'el here, Kea. There is no thought from him anywhere. Just look at it. He lets them die like the dogs they are… I almost feel sorry for them." Yeqon swept his hand out towards the valley below where bodies lay strewn everywhere, hacked or burned or both. "Women and children, that's all that's left." He cocked his ear, listening to their mourning ululations. "Do you think our dear I'el hears their cries?"

Kira's lashes glistened; her nostrils flared as her cheeks streamed with sadness.

"I don't understand, I'el called for Kea, told us to help… but we are…"

"Too late?" Yeqon sneered, "Of course, it's too late. He only seems to care in a timely manner if He thinks *we* are astray of our orders." Yeqon pulled another olive from the tree and squashed the fruit, golden oil slicked shiny along his fingertips.

"What should we do? Help the survivors?" Kira asked.

In a moment of silence, all three Watchers stared towards the horizon, at the blood, the char, the utter waste fading under a dusk sky.

"There is nothing here for us, nothing to salvage. A war has been fought and won, it's nothing we haven't done ourselves on a hundred other worlds, if you're to be honest," Yeqon said, and turned away, wings wide, ready to depart. "And don't forget, we must let them determine their own fate. Let today *be* that day." His eyes flickered skywards; his mouth pulled into a comfortable grimace.

"No!" Kea snapped. "We don't leave them here to be picked off, we will save who we can, take them back to your village, Yeqon. I'el does not want this population to diminish any further."

Yeqon's body tensed, his fingers clenched, he peered over his shoulder. "Well, they *have* diminished, haven't they?" He pointed sharply at the carnage across the valley floor. "And what would we do with them? Keep them under our wing? Hide them in the shadows where we must dwell? Once they know the truth of us, they can no longer live amongst their own kind, lest they share about us that which must not be known." He shook his head. "No, Kea, I'm not indulging I'el's idiocy this time by taking in the detritus of a world *He* created and abandoned."

"Yeqon! You can't leave them; you can't ignore their cries!" Kira said, her attention swept between him and the survivors whose mourning carried up the hill. She hugged the chill it brought to her skin.

"I can and I will leave them. My cries are ignored, so too can theirs be. There is nothing here for us. If you wish to join me, there is a feast at Jarmo, it's just north of Göbekli Tepe. You'll find it easily enough, Kira you remember the way. East side of the forest, second hill on the left. You'll hear us." He smiled, but there was no joy in his eyes.

Yeqon's wings flickered, he glared at Kira and Kea.

"Something is coming, and it isn't good. This place has a taste to it that I don't like. We best get away sooner rather than later or…" Yeqon sniffed; a breeze flicked through his long white hair. "Humans… they're stupid, selfish with a penchant for pointless violence. Violence should always have a purpose. I don't see how we can protect them from the shadows without exposing ourselves. It's going to be us or them in the end, and I promise you both this, I'll not choose them over myself if it comes down to survival. They aren't worth it." Yeqon snorted, tapped his hand to his Mark of A'vean and disappeared.

Chapter Eight

usk blushed a clear sky above Göbekli Tepe. The enormous standing stones sucked in the apricot hue of the sinking sun. Animal carvings adorning the sandstone shimmered like beacons as Yeqon disappeared within them.

Relief washed from his skin as he smelled a feast wafting from the underground city he'd called home for longer than he cared to dwell on. It had been better in the beginning when they were allowed to live closer to humanity, when the warmth of the sun and freshness of the wind lent him towards better moods.

"Mal'eus," Yeqon nodded at the sentry guarding the entrance.

"Yeqon, just in time. The feast is hot and plentiful," Mal'eus responded, a smile brightened the depths of his eyes, his mark glimmered momentarily.

"I'll save you a morsel," Yeqon slapped Mal'eus on the shoulder and chuckled. "You're off duty tomorrow, you will be top of the line for first meal."

Mal'eus rubbed his stomach and smiled wider. "One of the few things I enjoy about these bodies is the food."

The air cooled quickly as Yeqon descended through a narrow, hand carved walkway. Sconces burned at regular intervals, mainly to keep insects at bay. Quartzine lined the walls and striped the floor, imbued with A'vean power, its gentle white glow lit the underground of Göbekli Tepe with a lunar softness.

"Yeqon!" Asbel stood; mouth stuffed with honeyed berries as Yeqon rounded a corner into a large chamber. "Thought you would never make it, nearly had to ascend Pathos… he was eyeing your meal, and your woman." Asbel laughed, then elbowed Pathos who merely grimaced whilst quickly shoving food into his mouth until his cheeks bulged. He followed Asbel towards Yeqon.

Yeqon's mouth quirked. His pulse raced a little faster at the thought of the sustenance of all his desires.

"You should know better, Pathos," Yeqon grumbled. "Where are you two going?" he asked as both Asbel and Pathos righted their belts and retrieved their swords from hooks hewn into the wall.

"Nomads are getting a little too close. They've set up two beats from here, just going to move them on."

"Fear or adoration your weapon of choice tonight?" Yeqon asked, winking slyly at Asbel.

Asbel rubbed his chin, his mark glimmered, its light drew out the bright blue of his eyes. He smirked, then chuckled. "Both have their merits; adoration is always satisfactory, but in this case, a random blinding will keep them away longer. If they like us, they tend to stick like shit and I prefer not to be near them if I can help it."

Yeqon smiled. He liked Asbel's ethos.

"It will be as it should be done, Asbel. Quietly, peacefully," Pathos grumbled.

"Of course, absolutely," Asbel winked at Yeqon.

Both Watchers laughed. Pathos frowned at them and left ahead of Asbel.

"Get rid of them quickly and quietly." Yeqon's eyes flicked up, his lips pressed firm. "Best keep our methods on Earth between you and me, and no one else, Asbel."

Asbel nodded, understanding Yeqon's need to keep I'el and everyone else out of the loop. Yeqon side-eyed the exit, attention briefly upon Pathos. "Is he troubled?"

"He's fine, just too old to bother trying to skirt the rules. He's bored to ascension, but too tired to care. He'll do whatever I do, don't worry." Asbel nudged Yeqon with his elbow.

Yeqon slapped his hand into Asbel's, their fingers laced into a fist, he leaned forwards and shared a K'ufili with him. "Hurry back, I don't want to put up with Ged'erel on my own. I might ascend him for no other reason than his wining irritates me," Yeqon said.

Asbel chuckled, shook his head, touched the Mark of A'vean glowing on his face. The air plucked at Yeqon's skin and Asbel evaporated.

Yeqon stood a moment, fingertips rolling across his thumbs, his stomach growled. He pressed against the firmness of his abdomen. There was a hunger there that was beyond food and soon he knew, he would have to feed it as well.

Chapter Nine

Yeqon thumped the table with his fist and raised a cup. "Kea! Welcome to the shithole we call home." His eyes were glassy, his smile loosened as he toasted Kea and Kira. Mead drained, his cup was immediately replenished and he drank some more.

Yeqon belched, lurched to the left and pulled at the waist of his current human flame. She giggled and fell eagerly into him. She twirled her fingers through his chest hair, leaned in to nibble his ear. The woman fit snug on his lap; her long black hair curtained her face as she nuzzled him.

Yeqon tipped his head to the right, affording more skin for her mouth, smiling at Kea and Kira; it was lust, not shame that bloomed across his skin.

Kea lowered her drink, joy faded as her smile waned. She stared expressionless at him. Kira looked away, sipping her own drink.

What are you doing, Yeqon? It's hands off the humans. Kea spoke in his mind.

Yeqon snorted, pushed the human girl away. She stumbled before finding her feet, scowling at Yeqon and swearing in her local dialect.

"More mead." Yeqon thrust his cup into her hand. She rolled her eyes and slumped away to tend his request, her protestations louder.

I do nothing I'm not allowed to, Kea. Merely tending her health, ensuring she is safe, giving her purpose in this otherwise purposeless world. Yeqon responded; the corner of his mouth tugged into a half smile.

No fraternising, no breeding with the humans, no utilising them for carnal pleasure, don't you recall? And… no servitude! Kea slipped Kira's hand into her own, drew her towards a table. They sat down opposite Yeqon upon a bank of stone draped in linens. Immediately waited upon by humans laden with platters of fruits and nuts, cured beets and maize cakes, they both looked uncomfortable. Kea waved them away.

"I can tend myself, thank you," Kea said. The humans halted, looked at each other, peered over to Yeqon, discomfort widening their eyes. Yeqon nodded at them, they lowered the platters, left jugs for Kea and Kira to pour themselves. The humans bickered between themselves, rolled their hands over and over, stood awkwardly behind Kea and Kira, seemingly unsure what to do with themselves.

See, you've upset them now. Yeqon smirked. *They thrive on purpose, on rules and guidance. Can't at all think for themselves… hence why we were sent here.*

It's more than pouring a drink, Yeqon, and you know that. It's… it's the mortal sex, the risk of breeding is just too high. Kea admonished him, pouring herself mead. She drank long, then slammed the cup so hard the platters rattled. Kira startled, glanced between Kea and Yeqon, not privy to their conversation. She patted Kea's arm; her efforts didn't dull the rosy flush of anger smattering Kea's cheeks.

Calm down. Who is breeding with them? Pleasure can be many things Kea, as you well know. I have not sullied a single human. Yeqon's eyes lingered upon Kea's lips, slid to her chest, his mouth parted, a groan rumbled in his throat.

Kea's face flushed brighter; her lips whitened as she pressed them firm, before smirking back at him. *Pleasure is something I know well; I just can't seem to remember anything remotely like that with you!* She drew Kira's hand closer and threaded their fingers together.

Kira narrowed her eyes at Kea. "What is it?" she asked.

"Nothing, it's nothing, I'm just tired from my long journey here." Kea leaned into Kira, pecked her lips and smiled; her fingers pressed against her mouth to seal the sensation in place. "That feels…" Kea's voice faded.

"It feels very different in this form. Does it please you?" Kira asked.

Kea nodded, tipped Kira's chin up and kissed her again. Kea held the kiss longer this time, her hand ran the length of Kira's hair, cupping gently under the nape of her neck. Someone cleared their throat.

Kira pulled away; shyness stained her cheeks. Kea peered over her shoulder.

"Koi!" Kea slapped her hands against her cheeks and blushed.

"Do not let me interrupt your acclimatisation," Koi smiled broadly. "Although I feel that your host is perhaps a little put out." Koi's swirling rainbow eyes glittered a brighter hue as he nodded Yeqon's way.

Kea looked towards Yeqon, whose knuckles were white, fists pressed hard into the table. His mouth worked slowly on an over-chewed morsel.

"You!" A human girl halted, mead jug in hand. "Yes, you!" Yeqon wriggled his fingers at her. The girl set the mead in front of Ged'erel who grumbled at having to pour it himself. She dashed towards Yeqon, who swiftly pulled her into his lap and whispered into her ear. She giggled and slipped her hand towards his groin. Yeqon reclined, anger slipped from his face. He smiled at Kea, quirked his brows… a challenge.

Koi sighed. "Leave it, Kea. He has been here for so long, he skims the edge of the forbidden to keep boredom at bay, but he's no harm, not really," Koi said. "I'll leave you to relax." He bowed farewell, as was the way of the eastern provinces he had happily integrated into.

"Koi, stay. Please join us." Kira swept her arm towards a spare seat just as a human set down a new platter of food. She held her hand up. "Thank you. I assure you we can serve ourselves." The young man frowned, rubbed his hands on his hips, peered about the room as though not knowing what to do.

"Take your leave, young one. Thank you for your service," Kea said, allowing her mark to glow a little above a gentle smile. The man's eyes widened, he beamed, pressed his hands together and bowed profusely.

"Much honour, much honour," he said in his own language before reversing from the room, disappearing beyond a pillar where a musician strummed an instrument of wood and cow gut.

Koi quirked a brow as he settled next to Kea. "Yeqon still lording around as though he's a king, Kira?" Koi looked across to Yeqon, whose own steely gaze preceded a nod and raising of yet another full cup of mead.

"Koi! Kalor! Welcome." Yeqon called. His words bled together.

Koi returned the gesture, "Kalor, Yeqon." Koi drained his mead, wincing as he swallowed. "That could have done with a little longer on the shelf." He reached for water and downed that before plucking at some flat bread, pulling it apart, one mouthful at a time, one eye on Yeqon, his ear to Kea.

"When did you arrive, Kea?"

"Only a few hours ago, although I now see that I probably should have come earlier to sort his ego out. I should have taken any route, no matter how long or arduous." Kea nodded at Yeqon, who sucked on a stone fruit, sweeping his tongue across his lips to catch the juice. The woman in his lap moved behind him and began combing the length of his hair with her fingers.

"He's very comfortable despite the fact he seems to loathe the place," Kea added.

"He has never had trouble entertaining himself, despite his moaning," Koi replied. "And believe me, he moaned a lot when you didn't deploy with him years ago."

"Looks like he's coped just fine," Kea said.

"He resented you had a choice when he didn't." Koi swallowed the last of his bread.

"He should know why I made that choice. He needed time to think on his manners. It doesn't look like there's been much self-reflection," Kea responded with a sigh. "Shame, I know deep down there is something better in him."

A rush of tepid air tousled her hair, Kea turned around, along with Koi and Kira.

Yeqon banged his fist on his table and rolled his eyes. "Damned Pathos. Why are *they* here?" He clapped his cup down again. Mead sloshed across the table.

"Look away!" Yeqon yelled.

The human servers lowered their heads without hesitation, well trained to avoid the power of Watcher transference as the Eloi Council arrived on the breath of the next gust. A sharp flash of light and scorching heat preceded them.

Yeqon stood, rolled his shoulders, cracked his neck. He plastered a smile on his face and bowed. "Welcome wise ones. Come, eat, drink, rest." He pointed to spare seats in the bustling meal chamber. "Last meal is still being served." Yeqon clicked his fingers, "You, more music."

A woman in sable skins retrieved a delicately carved aulos, called for the other musician, and they both sat behind Yeqon on a smooth rocky dais. They began to play in tandem, a gentle music underpinning the chatter.

"Kalor Noris, Yeqon." Matias led the Eloi, Pathos at his back. "You forget the mother tongue?"

"Of course not. The colloquial languages wear upon us at times." Yeqon inclined his head. "Kalor Noris, Matias."

Yeqon accepted Matias' hand, and then a K'ufili. "You look well, ancient one," Yeqon said.

Matias' mouth quirked, his face an emotionless plane. He stepped aside as Pathos greeted Yeqon with a steely gaze before, Theus, Amais and Serail followed suit in the same manner as Matias.

Serail grasped Yeqon's arm a little longer than necessary, the veins in his arm pulsed white beneath smooth ebony skin. "Just because we were the first, you do not get to name call," Serail smiled. "Ancient ones… you arrived not long after us. You birthed only a millennium after the First," Serail laughed and slapped Yeqon on the shoulder, hesitantly accepting a cup pressed at him from a passing server. He did not drink.

"True, please sit. It has been an age since we feasted together." Yeqon moved so they could pass by to their seats, Matias eyeing the woman who lingered behind Yeqon. She would not meet his eyes, but dipped her head and slipped away, disappearing into the shadows of the chamber.

"Regale us of the first days," Yeqon said. "I am sure some here are less familiar. My memory is a blur of boredom. I would not do it justice. Tell me your story again."

"Come Yeqon, you can recall it well enough. Surely you have not failed to teach those who came after you of the history?" Amais asked.

Yeqon shrugged and slurped his drink. "Please, share what this world was like. Kea surely does not know?"

Kea, still stoney faced, shook her head. "Please, Amais, I would be honoured to hear about the efforts you have made."

Amais side-eyed Yeqon. "Very well. I will make it brief."

The chamber fell silent. "When humans were little more than a thought in I'el's great plan, there was a giant age as this planet bubbled and rumbled into shape. The seas rose and fell, froze and warmed. It was a time of strange and beautiful creatures, of wild weather, when the Earth was orbited by many a danger. It was left to stew in its own primordial soup, so to speak. It was not safe, so I'el watched it turn about its sun until it was battered by the tail of a great asteroid. The giant ones died away, the planet went dark, and it sat that way for so long even I cannot count the years. Yet, it was closely monitored, for it was a place of interest, far away from other more dangerous worlds, safe from the less savoury of species. A place I'el wished to start a new form of life, one in his image, in our image, one to thrive and do so under their own volition." Amais poured a cup of water, sipped it silently, the room hanging upon his every utterance. "Most here are privy to the failings of worlds such as Satanos," he looked unashamedly at Yeqon, who gulped another mead down in response to the unspoken barb.

"This world was to be different. So, when the skies cleared of corruption and we pulled the first humans from the swamps, a new set of rules was set into place and our mission was to see it adhered to." Amais pointed at Yeqon. "You, Yeqon, arrived not long after Satanos was sealed. Do you not recall how you laughed at the weakness of the first humans? You mocked their appearance, questioned the point of it all… dare I say, risked the wrath of I'el with your impertinence?" Amais said, waving away an offer of bread. A hushed whisper circled the chamber.

Yeqon's eyes narrowed, his nostrils flared as he drew breath and laughed his embarrassment away. He chuckled again after a long draught, his eyes now red-rimmed. "Indeed, the early humans were quite repulsive… now though, your work has honed them into a more agreeable form." His attention roamed the chamber, settling on the woman who had pandered to him earlier, who now attempted to serve food to the Eloi.

"And it is that attitude that brings us here, Yeqon. Your fraternizing and subjugation have not gone unnoticed," Theus' deep voice reverberated across the table. He did not eat either, instead, his fingers tapped upon the table, one finger finding a divot. He pressed into it until the pink of his finger pad blanched. "We come to bid you cease such arrogance, and tend your duty, which is to watch over the humans, not utilise them."

Yeqon stiffened, he set his mead down, he ran a finger around the rim of the cup. "I do nothing the humans do not wish to engage in. None are here against their will." He waved a hand around the room. "Ask any of them. They are most happy to be in our presence. We give them purpose; they repay that with comfort. This is a fair compromise when so many of us have been punished unjustly. Unable to seek the solace of our own homes, our own families, it is unbearable. Do we not deserve some small comforts?"

A moment of strained silence ensued. There was a truth in Yeqon's words, and he could see the unspoken acknowledgement in the shine of Amais' eyes. While some A'veans could come and go freely, others like Yeqon, the warriors of Satanos, were indefinitely separated from their homeland at I'el's pleasure.

Serail rubbed his chin, nodding. "It is a punishment most difficult, Yeqon, that I most assuredly understand. I too have not seen A'vean for longer than my memory serves."

"At your choice, Serail. It was your choice to stay… not mine!" Yeqon thumped the table again. Kira winced; Kea stared cooler than ever.

"Show me one human who doesn't want to be near us. They adore us. I'm just letting nature take its course, not interfering in *their* choices… as dearest Father has directed." Yeqon smiled. His lips quivered over his teeth.

"Of course, humans will adore us, Yeqon. They are dazzled, overwhelmed, and that is exactly why you must leave them be. They do not understand what they are dealing with. They cannot consent to the danger we pose." Theus' voice deepened, his mark flared a little too brightly, and the humans grabbed their eyes. "Be off, all of you," Theus commanded, thrusting his arm towards the entrance. Platters fell and mead vats tumbled as every last human scattered towards the exit. The smell of their fear stained the air.

Yeqon's jaw feathered, one hand balled into a fist. "That food could have fed those humans you care so much for," he said, pointing to the spilled platters.

"And that's how little you value them? Scraps from the ground?" Matias narrowed his eyes. The depth of his skin seemed to darken even further with the shadow of anger. "You over step, Yeqon. You have taken liberties where the rest of us have bided our time in the dreams of humanity, as we were instructed."

Yeqon huffed, stood and retrieved the last urn of mead. The room was silent but for liquid pouring into his now cracked cup. The honeyed liquor beaded out and seamed down the side, coursed his forearm and dripped onto the floor. His hungry gulps curled Serail's lips and thinned Theus' eyes further.

Yeqon belched, peered into the emptiness of his cup, then threw it against the wall. It smashed, he nodded and sat back down.

"Whilst I appreciate the effort of a visit by the most revered council of Eloi, I can assure you all, I know all too well where the line is. It hits me in the face daily. I admit I teeter on it, often I feel compelled to fall right over it…" Yeqon belched again. Kea screwed up her face and shook her head at him.

"I am often tempted to do whatever pleases me, but I don't. I respect the Throne just enough. I do not breed with them. I'el forbid the kind of abomination that would produce!" Yeqon's face crinkled, his lip curled away from his teeth. "I'd not demean our lineage with such a destiny."

"Perhaps," Theus said. "But you push the limits too far, treat the humans with disdain, and it must stop before the moon reaches its zenith this day. You must no longer be seen or heard by humans after the sun rises tomorrow."

"Then how am I to…"

Yeqon was cut off by a soul-crushing wail. The cavern chatter stilled, not a breath drawn as all present looked up, the sound penetrating from above-ground. The wail intensified, it clung to the air, seemed to hook itself to each Watcher, stir their power to life.

The cavern glowed white with an instant, nervous energy.

"What is this?" Ged'erel, quiet in his misery until now, pulled himself up.

The Eloi gathered close, all five with their attention focused upwards, listening to the outside world.

Yeqon grabbed the closest wall as the ground shook. He rocked on his feet. Cups fell and rolled across the floor. Every Watcher released their wings and reached for a weapon. Yeqon pushed through them, past the Eloi. His waning, perpetual scowl gave way to wide-eyed alarm. He stopped in the middle of his kindred, eyes following a fissure's appearance in the ceiling. It threaded quickly through the sandstone, opening wider with another quake. His fingers flexed, the veins in his arms glimmered iridescent; sweat glistened across his skin. Yeqon took a step towards the exit, but halted when the wailing stopped. His upper lip twitched and a bead of sweat steamed as it coursed from his forehead through his Mark of A'vean.

"The Göbekli Portal is active, and it's not one of us," Matias said. "What have you done, Yeqon?"

"Nothing!" Yeqon answered through gritted teeth. He moved closer to the exit; Pathos swept his hand across Yeqon's chest.

"Wait," he commanded. Yeqon obeyed, the strange energy in the air, the vibration of Göbekli, had his heart thumping uncomfortably.

"Weapons at the ready," Serail said, and all present held aloft a chromious sword or dagger, the cavern further alight.

Hurried footsteps filled the void of their silent anticipation. The wailing stopped as suddenly as a heart staked with a knife. All turned towards the entrance, to the pounding vibration of feet. Yeqon's fingers whitened around the pommel of his sword. His nostrils flared, and he sniffed. "Blood…" The wail pierced the air again, followed by another quake. All wavered on their feet, eyes wide with confusion. Yeqon glanced nervously around the cavern, tongue sweeping across his lips.

"What is happening? asked Kira

"I don't know," Kea said, a tremor in her voice.

The ground shifted again… and a baby wailed.

The Eloi looked at each other, Theus' eyes fell heavily upon Yeqon.

"What… have… you… done?"

Chapter Ten

ea and Kira disappeared up the corridor. Yeqon squared off with Theus.

"What have *I* done?" Yeqon thumbed his own chest. "The earth quivers and you immediately look to me? After I gave you my honesty?" His voice was gravel. It hitched. "I know as much as you, Theus!" He looked back to the corridor, those footsteps neared.

What have you done? Kea whispered in his mind.

Yeqon stepped towards the corridor, but halted. "I haven't done…" His words petered out when Kea and Kira reappeared.

"By the Throne, no!" Amais said. "This cannot be."

The energy in the cavern dulled as the Eloi gathered around Kea. She held a human woman in her arms. But it was what Kira held that rooted them all to the spot. Everyone looked at Yeqon.

Yeqon's blood ran cold. Smug anger left his face flat, his mouth gaping with shock, and his hand slid limply from his sword. He paled. "This was not me; I swear on the Throne, I did not do this!"

"In the name of I'el..." Serail said. "...this should not be so." He moved towards Kea and pressed his palm against the pallor of the human's cheek. "Put the woman over there. Stand down." He waved at everyone else, then inspected what Kira held. Serail shook his head, ran a hand down his face, and sighed.

"And for all we have done, for all we have sacrificed, it comes to this," he said.

The infant in Kira's arms cried, and as though the Earth heard, the cavern rumbled again. Kira shielded the babe from a spray of dirt, held it close, rocked side to side until it quieted.

Yeqon backed away. He remained silent, licking his lips over and over, unable to find enough moisture, trying to settle the acid in his throat. A new, thicker sweat broke across his brow.

Theus wandered towards the human woman. Kea gently tended her, removing the afterbirth, pulsing light over the woman's abdomen to settle her bleeding. The woman groaned, her eyes rolled back and unconsciousness claimed her.

"Bring it here," Kea called Kira over. "It needs its mother."

Kira moved, but Theus stood in her way. His breadth stopped her in her tracks.

"We cannot let this go any further, Kira. She must know nothing, remember nothing. This..." He jerked his head at the infant. "This being cannot ever know what it is, cannot ever be replicated. It should be erased immediately."

"It's not a thing, Theus! It most certainly will not see any harm." Kira recoiled from him. "It is innocent. Its creation is the fault of one of us. Let it not suffer for the sin of another." Kira stared hard at Theus, her mark glimmered in warning. She then skirted him and laid the babe in Kea's arms. Kea leaned forwards, shifted the mother's robes and set the babe to her swollen breast. Nature guided the child, and it nursed noisily. The mother roused and groaned, but did not open her eyes. Her legs began to shake, then her entire body. Kea quickly lifted the child away, Kira taking it again.

"Oh no," Kea said as blood pooled between the woman's legs.

The quiet of the cavern ceased as the Watchers began whispering among themselves, attention heavy upon the scene before them. Nervous tension bit the air, the static of their power tugged their hair, it streaked overhead and drew gooseflesh to their skin.

The Eloi gathered closer to Kea, all glaring at the mother and the Nephilim child.

"Who is responsible for this?" Matias asked. "Who condemns humanity?" He peered over his shoulder at Yeqon.

"It *wasn't* me!" Yeqon snapped. "I've never seen that human before. There are thousands of them. They're like vermin, breeding everywhere. I don't know them all, Matias and I definitely don't know that one!" He pointed sharply, repeatedly. "It was not me!"

"Well, someone does know who she is, and they have known her in a way they should not have. I..." Matias rocked as the cavern shook heavily. The seam overhead opened a foot wide; dirt rained over them. Watchers began to cough in the thickening air.

"Retreat! We will deal with this elsewhere," Matias ordered. One by one, the Watchers transferred from the crumbling cavern. Yeqon lagged behind, eyes heavily on Kea who scooped the woman up in her arms, Kira taking the infant.

Kea looked nervously at Kira. "I don't think I can transfer a human."

Yeqon held out his arms. "Give her to me." Kea was about to hesitate, but the floor of the cavern opened up, and she was too new to visualise somewhere to transfer to.

"Come on!" Yeqon shook his arms impatiently.

"Give her to him, Kea. It's okay," Kira said. Kea slipped the woman into Yeqon's protection. She held his arm, one hand upon Kira, and they transferred away barely seconds before the cavern collapsed.

Chapter Eleven

The world was on fire. Yeqon trailed Kea on foot, threading through the pillars of Göbekli Tepe, out across the grassy plains that capped their underground home. Char filled each breath. The air burned down his throat. He scooped up a fleeing human by the arm and took to the air. The man dangled precariously below him, like an eagle with its prey. Yeqon flew beyond the portal, across the peak of a craggy, rock-strewn hill to the north, following the excrement smell of fear-ridden humans.

"Run!" He growled and dropped the man who dared not look back, but scrambled onto wobbly legs, chasing hurried footprints. The earth rumbled, the human fell, got up and tumbled down the far side of the hill as the ground shifted more violently.

"Fuck!" Yeqon looked up. The sky roiled. Something flickered beyond the thick blanket of clouds. Something was beyond their angry churning, something or someone was on its way.

"What? What is it now?" He screamed to the sky, his face illuminated, his muscles sharpened. His innards felt tight and uncomfortable under his skin. Something beyond his control relinquished Yeqon to an unusual feeling… fear.

Yeqon took a burning breath and flew back towards Kea and Kira, crossing paths with dozens of his own kind who dashed about picking up humans, risking themselves against something unseen, something absolutely not of this world.

What's going on? Mind chatter was chaos. He couldn't understand what anyone was saying.

Göbekli Tepe burned a bright orange under a great wall of fire that had set the distant forest alight; a hellish, haloed smudge on the horizon. Göbekli Tepe's portal light stuttered, the hum of it like nails drawn across a rock. The sky glimmered; bruised clouds roiled under a hungry wind.

"What's going on?" Kira yelled over the howling.

"I… don't… Oh no!" Kea looked up; the clouds peeled away as though melting from the sky.

"Yeqon! *Is* this your doing?" Kea screamed at him as he looked up, his face fell, his breaths quickened, and for a singular moment, terror iced his veins and blurred his vision with tears. He stared at a widening aperture opening between Earth and the universe. He sucked a deep breath, bit his lip so hard that blood trickled down his chin. His eyes widened as four bright lights appeared, rapidly growing larger by the second. He drew another breath, now anger churned beneath his skin, the heat of resentment dried his eyes.

"No! I told you, Kea… I didn't lay with that woman! I have never lain with any human in *that* way!" Yeqon yelled, teeth bared, spittle foaming in the corners of his mouth.

They all ducked as the windstorm drove biting sand into their flesh.

"What do we do?" Kira cried, hugging the now screaming infant closer to her chest.

Theus appeared behind her. He pointed sharply upwards. "We run, we hide, we hope to see the light of another day before they arrive!" Theus peered skywards again; the four glimmering lights grew bigger, more luminous by the second. He pushed Kea on, out of the shadow of Göbekli Tepe. One of its great pillars fell, the crack of it jolted through Yeqon.

Theus shoved him in the back as he urged them all into the sky, towards the fire of the horizon. Kira and Yeqon trailed protectively behind Kea, who struggled under the weight of the limp mother as the sky ripped at them from every side. The ground rumbled and ripped apart far below. Great fissures gaped, sucking trees and fire and people into the belly of the earth. They couldn't help those ones; they could only help themselves in this moment. They flew faster, ducking debris that spun along the violent winds.

Kea swayed out of the way of a flying branch; she tumbled backwards, nearly losing grip of the mother. Yeqon dipped and grabbed her hand until she righted herself.

"Are you alright?" he asked.

Kea nodded. "For now. Thank you," her voice laboured as she flew on. Kea pulled up suddenly though, hovering, battered by the buffeting gale.

"Hurry on!" Theus called back.

"Wait…" Kea felt wetness against her skin, padded her hand along the mother's body. The mother's robes darkened crimson; blood oozed anew, hot and sticky against Kea's body.

"Oh, no!" Kea searched desperately below, looking for somewhere safe to land.

"Leave her Kea!" Yeqon said.

"No, I won't," Kea plummeted. Kira and Theus followed. Yeqon hesitated, looked up. Those lights were even closer. "Shit, shit!" He hovered alone in the wildness of the sky as the others disappeared below. His eyes dashed left and right. He coughed on the ash of each breath, his skin slick with it. He thought of heading straight up, deep into the vastness of the universe, far away from Earth. His wings moved, he coasted higher, but the clouds filled with lightning, their thunder sent him tumbling backwards, and those bright lights clawed a dread through his gut.

"Argh!" Yeqon dropped, scanned the ground and found three shapes under the shadow of a cliff that overhung the river that fed the valley. His feet hit the ground. It was hot, unsettled, as he made his way to where Kea had set the mother down. She leaned across her body and shielded the mother as best she could as the wind pressed in mercilessly.

"Is she dead?" Yeqon asked, impatience sharpened his voice.

"Not yet," Kea coughed on the ash-filled air. Her fingers trailed the duskiness of the mother's lips. Kea's hand came away wet, the touch of impending death leaving the mother's skin cold and sweaty. The woman's breaths were shallow and rapid. Kea lit her hand, held it over the mother's heart…

The infant cried. Kira gently pressed the crook of her little finger to its lips, and it sucked contentedly for the time being.

"Let her go, we are in danger," Yeqon reached for Kea, but she elbowed him away. "No!"

Her hand pulsed again over the mother's heart as blood stained the rubble dark underneath.

"Come now lady, your babe needs you, come now…" Kea's voice hitched as Theus' fingers curled around her wrist.

"Enough, Kea. Nature has made a choice, and now we must make one to save what's left of this atrocity and ourselves before our fate is decided for us." Sweat beaded like diamonds down the brown of his cheeks, he glanced again at the lights in the sky that were closer by the second.

Kea's light faded as Theus pulled her up and away from the mother. He pushed her past Yeqon, towards Kira. Buffeted by the wind, Kea stared at the mother as she gasped, drawing no more breath. Her body twitched. She went slack, her skin immediately paled, as though life had never coursed through it at all. The infant cried. Kea hugged into Kira, both Watchers protecting the Nephilim child.

The Earth moaned, its voice a desperate howl beneath their feet. The ground shuddered with displeasure as the sky opened up further, those lights bigger and bigger. The cliff began to crumble. Rose-streaked debris pelted all four of them. Kea wrapped her wings around Kira, shielding her with her own body and wings as the clouds drew away from an ever-darkening aperture and ominous arrival.

Yeqon enveloped Kea, Kira, and the Nephilim. Theus helped no one.

"Is it them?" Kira cried, coughing on thicker, burning air.

Theus nodded sharply. "If you wish to remain intact, I suggest you give me the child and flee."

Kira hesitated; the infant close to her breast, a flush of colour stained her cheeks.

"Please, it's so innocent." Kira's eyes set her misery free as Kea gently drew the infant from her. "It's the only way. We have no chance against them," Kea said as she looked up through her wings. The four lights were now blinding. "Theus is right."

"Listen to her Kira, we are ash if we don't do as Theus says," Yeqon hacked on a fresh gust of boiling air.

Kira nodded; she sniffed back sorrow as she relinquished the swaddling still bunched in her fist. She looked down at the child, her eyes still misted, and she kissed its head as it wailed until its lips quivered. "I am sorry for this; you are but an innocent one in a world of violence."

Kea passed the child to Theus and drew Kira close to her side. Her wing wrapped around Kira.

Theus looked grimly at Yeqon. "Take it." He passed the baby to Yeqon, his arms awkward around the tiny crying half-human as it settled against his chest.

"What am I to do with this?" Yeqon asked, eyes flicking skyward; retribution was on its way. His heart beat too fast, his mind a clutter. He could almost feel the weight of I'el's hand upon him.

"You say you're not responsible, Yeqon. You may not have made this Nephilim child, but you didn't discourage the behaviour amongst your brethren, to the many who have looked up to you. You sowed the seed; you now reap the harvest of your miscalculation."

Yeqon's mouth opened to retort. Words of rebuttal died on his tongue. He looked to the sky again as a great horn boomed from the heavens. Yeqon's muscles felt like they might melt from his bones.

"Fuck!" his voice stuttered. He struggled to swallow as the horn reverberated through the skies again. Its song strummed the ground, plucked at the very core of the planet, and the four of them swayed.

"By the Throne!" Kea yelled.

"The Heralds! It's the Heralds! Get out now if you can!" Yeqon yelled as all four speared upwards, heading for the portal. They pulled up just as quickly upon seeing the great stones of Göbekli Tepe shifting. The light of its portal flickered on and off; its power diminished as its alignment deteriorated.

"No! No!" Yeqon yelled, spinning around, realising all too quickly that it was just him, Theus, Kea and Kira. Everyone else had disappeared. The Heralds' horn sounded again, thunder cracked overhead, and the wind renewed its power. All struggled to stay in control as great gusts buffeted them relentlessly. The infant squealed in Yeqon's arms.

"What do I do with this!" he growled at Theus.

"By the span of a day, there is a remote village south of here. By a river with a fig orchard. Find a human family with an infant, leave the Nephilim with them." He leaned into Yeqon, finger pointing sharply at his face. "They are to know nothing of this child other than it is an orphan. They are not to know who or what you are. They are not to know it is a bastard that should never have been. Get it done and get yourself to safety if you value your existence." Theus pointed up.

"All has been seen, all shall be undone. We are at His mercy." Theus touched his Mark of A'vean and transferred away.

"Wait! Theus? Don't leave us!" Kira screamed, but Theus was gone, a mere echo upon the ether. Kea tried to calm her, but Kira wailed. "This can't be. It just can't be happening. We have done all that we were asked to do," Kira sobbed as Kea protected her from the violence pushing at them.

Yeqon struggled with the screaming infant, his wings pumped hard, angling this way and that to maintain his balance.

"He left us, that bastard left us!" Yeqon's chin quivered; it was not fear that snaked through his veins, it wasn't fear that left his arms almost too tight around the infant. He looked down at it. "Hush, hush, you have done enough." It continued its wailing.

"Yeqon?" Kea called.

"Yeqon, what do we do?" Kea's voice was faint; muted by the chaos trying to pull them from the skies. Yeqon drew his eyes from the

Nephilim. The endless night of the universe peered down at them, the sun bowed away, its strength no longer enough to light the Earth. Stars moved in the darkness overhead, zipping fast across the velvet of it. Those four lights, the Heralds, were no longer alone.

"No… no you wouldn't?" Yeqon's chest felt too tight, his mind fogged. "Father, no!" He looked to his left. Kea's eyes met his, tears ran freely, unashamedly. She had seen them, too.

Yeqon drew a deep breath and yelled. "Kea… get away now!" He backed away from the Arc Angels rapidly descending towards Earth; their arrival announced with another call of the Heralds' horns.

"Get away, Kea! Go now, take Kira…" Yeqon yelled, "…go home, go back to A'vean!" He backed away, eyes wide and red-rimmed as he stared up at Armageddon.

The most powerful and dangerous angels of A'vean were descending rapidly towards them.

Kea's mouth hung; shock held her still as she understood the sight. Her wing light faltered, and she dipped suddenly as she tried to take flight directly into the raging storm.

"They wouldn't …" she gasped, unable to take her eyes from the terrifying sight of Arc Angels.

"Yes, they would dispatch you in an instant just for being in their way," Yeqon yelled over the cacophony overwhelming the Earth. He retreated higher up, stretching his wings wider, pumping hard as he struggled to stay aloft against the chaos.

Kea's grip slid down Kira's arm, she only just caught hold of Kira's hand; their fingertips blanched as they struggled to hold onto each other. "We can't leave humans to their wrath! They won't stand a chance," Kea cried.

Kira nodded. "We *must* help the humans." She managed to pull closer to Kea, and they scanned the burning earth below.

"At your own peril, then," Yeqon yelled, his words muted by the raging storm and the cries of the Nephilim. As Kea and Kira screamed for him to stop, he turned away, babe pressed at his chest. Yeqon flew into the gusts of the storm, squinted at the bite of sand smacking into his face, shuddered at the burning ash searing into his skin. The Heralds' horn called a final time, its power tossed him through the air. When he regained his balance, infant still screaming, he spun back to see the first Arc Angel hit the ground.

Chapter
Twelve

The earth shuddered as the first of four Arc Angels hit the ground. A wave of energy rolled through the air, knocking Yeqon off course, making him tumble a dozen times, nearly dropping the slippery newborn. It wailed louder and louder; the sound turned his blood to ice. If those angels saw him with it, he would be nothing more than a mere memory.

Yeqon righted himself, stopped to find his bearings, and found a small spot of earth far below. He landed atop a peaked ridge in the middle of the forest. The trees burned so fiercely it blistered his skin, the black smoke of it drew water to his eyes. He caught his breath, tried to clear his thoughts, but the sounds of the Arc Angels baring their wrath upon the Earth loosened his stomach… he vomited. The Nephilim screamed.

With acid coating his throat, Yeqon ducked under a long-dead tree, its ancient skeleton only just catching alight as embers flew by upon the wind. Behind the expanse of its grey trunk, he jiggled the babe uselessly, trying to settle it as he'd seen human women do. It wailed even louder.

"Stop it! This is all your doing!" Yeqon's hand hovered over its face, the temptation to silence it forever made his fingers tremble. His thumb grazed its tiny mouth, his hand twitched, his eyes flicked back to the tooth-like shadow of Göbekli Tepe in the distance. He held his breath, dulled his power to almost nothing, and watched those four Arc Angels circle the ancient portal. They guarded the way out, the way home; the portal whose light had gone dark.

Arc Angels were enormous. They stood ten feet tall, beings of pure light, bringers of justice, purveyors of I'el's divine intervention. Yeqon licked his lips, tasted the salt of fear upon them. He wasn't ready to become a memory and felt the injustice of a punishment he did not deserve. He looked at the newborn that screamed until its tongue was tinged blue. His huge hand could crush it in a breath, he could put an end to the whole mess, deny he knew anything of it. But as his small finger pressed temptingly against the infant's mouth, he drew a breath of surprise.

The babe latched onto his knuckle, its little lips warm and hungry against his skin. It sucked eagerly for sustenance, found none, but was contented in the moment with the comfort of the connection. Yeqon stared at the tiny Nephilim, tipped his head, his cheek twitched, the corner of his mouth curled ever so slightly.

"Hmph, if only you knew how much you are not worth my mercy." He pulled the babe closer to his chest, secure and warm, safe in the arms of imminent danger. The ground shuddered again, the ancient tree cracked, split by lightning. He launched up as the firestorm rushed through where he had sat only moments ago. The surrounding earth burned to ash.

The air was thick with the smell of death and it buzzed with an intoxicating, terrifying energy. The power of the Arc Angels snaked and snapped over his head, underneath his feet… everywhere. It was an interstellar lightning that held the message of obliteration and sent a new course of dread through his veins.

The way ahead was thick and black. He could no longer see the Arc Angels, but he could hear their roar, feel the pain of their power, and that fanned a panic that sucked the breath from his lungs.

They screamed, they bellowed the ancient language across the plains of the Earth, a great thunder of accusation to all Watchers. He didn't want to acknowledge the words, didn't want to see what they were doing, but Yeqon couldn't help himself. He needed to know what was happening, how he could save himself.

Whilst the Nephilim was quiet, he flexed his wings, lifted up just high enough to see past the burning blanket of the forest. The air still thick and hot, he coughed and retched again. When his eyes cleared, and the hacking ceased, he found a small patch of clear sky, an eye through to the world below.

"By the Throne… no!" He whispered.

The Arc Angels circled Göbekli Tepe, charred marks left in the wake of their ethereal footprints. They called their ancient song again; it raked across Yeqon's skin. A scattering of humans appeared, fleeing their hiding places dotted around Göbekli Tepe. They dashed across the burning landscape, fled the otherworldly creatures, screaming… stupidly announcing their location.

An angel turned, its silvery face creased, its eyes so blue, so cold and pure with the power of I'el, that even Yeqon had to look away. When he peered up again, the angel knelt to the ground, drew a great sword of light from its side and plunged it into the ground.

The world reverberated once more. Flames erupted from the Arc Angel's chromious weapon. They fanned across the landscape, a great orange wall snuffing out the humans in a tidal wave of heat. Blackness webbed across the ground in its wake, it seared quickly, had reached the humans in the time it took Yeqon to draw a breath.

"By the Throne… you wouldn't?" Yeqon whispered. The humans were engulfed and vaporised… gone as if they had never existed.

"You did… you actually did."

Chapter
Thirteen

Yeqon had watched in horror, the destruction, the utter razing of Göbekli Tepe. He had always known the wrath of I'el was something to behold, but as he hid within the clouds of detritus above the still-burning forest, he felt for the first time the sheer helplessness of being on the other side of that rage… and it stirred something dark within him.

The Arc Angels had circled for a few hours, searching for laggers, taking out errant Watchers as they tried fruitlessly to flee. It took just one look, one wave of their hand, and anything that caught their attention was non-existent before they could even comprehend death was upon them. The Arc Angels had retreated when all that spoke in the world below was the crackling, sizzling fodder of the flames. They'd left behind a war zone hidden within a haze of dust and smoke. Even with his immaculate sight, Yeqon could not fully appreciate the destruction.

He retreated as soon as it was safe, once the Heralds' horns were a memory. The sight of the Arc Angels was a nightmare he wished to forget. He flew south as fast as he could. The babe had begun crying again as he jostled it awkwardly, trying to keep its weight from pressing against painful blisters where ash had burned across his torso. He flew higher, letting the colder, thinner air tend the sting. He could smell the roast of his own flesh; he could feel his very soul burning at the thought of what the Arc Angels had done to the humans and his kindred.

"Protect humans," he spat at the wind. "But murder them yourself?" Yeqon shook his head; disgust whipped his speed along. "I followed your rules...." He flew on, powered by rage, not slowing until a dawning sun kissed the horizon, and the snaking tail of the great river appeared below. He coasted along its winding course until he found the smudge of orchards along its banks. Yeqon scanned the landscape that skirted the orchards and banked left. He began a slow descent, his attention constantly on the lookout, ears pricked just in case the horns began again.

The infant had succumbed to exhaustion, a tiny warmth tucked snuggly under his right arm. As his feet hit the ground, the moon sunk away, and a line of orange struck the horizon. The air still held the taste of fire, even so very far away, and Yeqon tried to spit it out, but it seemed imbedded upon his tongue.

The smell of death remained upon each breath, but the smoke, the fire, at least no longer ate at his skin. Yeqon rubbed his forehead, circled his temples with his fingers, and drew a deep breath before making his way to the edge of a tiny village. Dawn held a silence but for the squark of a rooster and the cackle of hens. A mangy dog sniffed around the shadowed outskirts; its eyes shone bright yellow at him. It growled at his presence. Yeqon hissed at it and it yelped, tail between its legs. It disappeared.

Yeqon walked on cautiously, his feet padding noiselessly. He held his breath lest he wake the babe. Passing a well, he rounded a tie-up holding two horses. They bobbed their heads and snorted in alarm as he came up behind them. He half-smiled, and lay a gentle hand upon the neck of a scruffy brown pony. "One of the few creations of worth," he whispered.

"Settle." His hand smoothed along its back, and he nodded to himself. He liked horses, useful creatures without the attitude of the A'vean Pegasus. They could argue a Watcher into oblivion. He circled his hand upon the pony's rump as it settled.

"Good boy." Satisfied they would remain silent, he left the horses, following the crackle of burning hearths that still warmed the occupants until the cold bite of night lost its sharpness.

He counted five dwellings, deciding to head to the one furthest from the others. It was the largest, perhaps belonging to the leader of the village.

A baby's cry broke the silence as he passed the first dwelling. Yeqon stopped, cocked an ear to the wooded wall.

"Lilith! For the love of the Gods, quiet!" A coarse female voice whisper-shouted. Something banged, and the infant named Lilith cried louder.

"Shut that thing up!" A male bellowed. There was another bang.

Lilith cried on, seemingly untended.

Yeqon peered down at the Nephilim that was settled in his arms. He hesitated, but then felt the hint of A'vean energy in the echo of its soul. He shook his head. "No, you get one chance, but not with them."

He padded quietly away, in his mind calling to his kindred.

Ged'erel? Kea? Silence echoed through his mind. Yeqon continued on past the rest of the homes until he came upon the last one, the dwelling farthest from where the poor Lilith child still howled. He rounded a thatch-roofed building until he found a window with nothing but a shadowed fallow field at his back. He cocked an ear, then peered into the small window. His cheek twitched; he loosened his grip on the child. For a human dwelling, it was neat, smelled relatively clean. The occupants were still asleep. All was quiet, other than the reverberating snore of a man.

Hmmm, lucky for you. He thought as he looked down at the Nephilim. A cradle sat inside by the hearth. This hut had a child too, a calm, sleeping one; a loved child. They would take it in, they *had* to take it in.

Yeqon set the infant down just outside the door. He knocked loud enough to both wake the occupants and set the Nephilim to scream.

He quickly transferred away, hiding himself a hundred feet within the fig orchard to the right of the field.

There was a commotion. The door rattled as it was unlatched. A bearded man looked around the edge of the doorway, spear in hand, rubbing tiredness from his eyes until they widened with clarity. The crying infant at his feet immediately caught his attention. He stared a moment, maybe longer. He leaned down, flicked the swaddling aside.

"Mariam!" he called, looking back up, wariness now coloured those weary eyes. He stared into the shadows of the orchard, looking directly at Yeqon, but not seeing him at all.

The door opened wider. A woman appeared. "What is it, Josa?" she asked, yawning.

"Look," Josa said, pointing down.

"Oh! Oh no! Poor dear!" Mariam's mouth gaped. She kneeled and scooped up the Nephilim child, an experienced sway to her body, immediately settling it. It snuggled into the comfort of her arms.

"Who could have left a child to the weather?" Mariam's face furrowed, her hands quickly unwrapping the swaddling. "A boy. Josa, it's a boy!" She smiled, lifting the infant up, nuzzling her lips to its cheeks. She lowered it down again, pushed her robe aside and the Nephilim infant immediately sought the comfort of her milk-swollen breast.

Within the home, another child cried.

"A friend for Eve." Mariam smiled, angling her body for Josa to see the infant that had drawn a blush of joy to her cheeks. Josa didn't smile, his attention still on the landscape, eyes narrowed.

"Go back inside," he said. Mariam did as he instructed.

"Eve, darling daughter, you have a friend. Thank the Gods," Mariam said. The song of her voice carried all the way to Yeqon.

Yeqon kept his eye on Josa.

Josa retrieved a torch from within the home, held its burning flame aloft, and circled the dwelling. He sniffed the air, narrowed his eyes at birds fleeing from the north. He stared at the sky a while before going back inside and latching the door.

Yeqon waited until the movements in the house settled before he eased back to the hut and listened in.

"I'm not sure we can keep him," Josa said.

"Oh please, Josa? Someone left him with us for a reason. He is a gift from the Gods for us," Mariam said, her voice strained with pleaded. "For so long we were not blessed with a child, and now we have two."

There was silence.

"Please Josa?"

Silence again.

"Very well, but be certain that if the parents call for it, we give it back?"

"Very well," Mariam answered. "Until then, I will call him Ahdem."

Worry not, lady, I will not be calling on you again.

Yeqon withdrew, needing to hear no more. He had placed the infant away from danger, as Theus had ordered. Now he needed to find sanctuary for himself. He looked up; the sky was clear, A'vean upon his mind.

Breaking through the fig trees, he quickly breached a thin smear of cloud; the crisp left overs of night almost fooling him into believing all was well. He coasted easily on a light breeze, intent on staying south, finding another portal and seeing the back of this world he hated more today than ever. But something held his attention, something gnawed at him. He kept looking back over his shoulder, kept calling for Ged'erel, for Kea, Kira and Asbel; even for Theus.

"Argh!" Fear tightened his belly, his eyes so wide they pained. He turned back and flew north, even though instinct told him danger lurked in that direction. He travelled until the air became thicker with smoke, until he could taste death richly on each breath, until the amber glow of a burning world lit the way.

Yeqon dropped to the ground south of Göbekli Tepe, or what felt like Göbekli Tepe. The ground his feet sunk into felt and looked nothing like it. The earth was hot between his toes, some areas burned shiny and hard, the ground glimmered like a mirrored lake.

Kea? Kira? Ged'erel? Theus? No one answered his calls. No animal growled, no bird chirped, not so much as an ant crawled.

Yeqon was airborne again. He moved slowly, as though the air were honey. Each beat of his wings was sheer agony, searching for someone, for anyone. He turned left; he turned right; he spun on the spot a dozen times, glistening diamond skeletons dotting the landscape. The sky flashed here and there. Souls… Watcher souls were everywhere. They dashed about after mortal death, confused and lost. Yeqon called to them as they scattered through the atmosphere, blue streaks of desperation separated from their flesh and bone.

Yeqon's breaths became harder, faster, shallow and sharp. His skin prickled as he took in the carnage, breathed in the odour of dead Watchers, and felt the sharp cut of their disorientation.

Kea? Asbel? He looked to the fading stars, calling again for *their* souls. *Ged'erel? Theus?* No one answered.

Yeqon's eyes thinned. They stung red and raw. Misery trailed down his ash-stained face, silver lines in the wake of his tears.

"I'el! Where are they?" Wind whipped his unanswered question away. His teeth ground, every muscle rigid.

"*Where* are they?" he screamed. No one answered. The Earth echoed his pain back at him.

Chapter
Fourteen

Yeqon stood on a rise to the north of Göbekli Tepe. Blood crusted in his nails, his fingers unwinding from fists, eight crescents sliced into his palms. Clouds still surged, cumulous and dark, blotting out a new dawn. The air gasped, tugged at his air, nipped at his skin. The portal was dead, its light a memory, its power a myth.

The world was silent. Yeqon slowly backed away, wings widening, and he lifted into the air. He reached for a surging gust and let it drive him away from the carnage, from the slaughter of his own… by his own. He tapped his Mark of A'vean and arrived back at the northern portal to find that henge dull as well. Its stones turned over, the ground scorched … dozens of human corpses blackened to char at its base.

Blue lights streaked haphazard through the sky, just as they did over Göbekli Tepe. A'vean souls, mortal bodies destroyed. They darted here and there, looking for a way home, but there was none.

"What have you done?" Yeqon's words were weak. There was no fight in them.

Yeqon touched his mark again, intent on heading to another portal, to get off this planet before he too, was trapped like those insipid souls above. But when he found himself in transit somewhere over the great Southern Ocean, he quite suddenly lost his way. He pulled up, hovered, looked left and right, plucked at his beard. He shook his head, tried to clear his thoughts, which felt unexpectedly thick and foggy. For some reason, Yeqon did not know which way to go.

"What is going on?" Yeqon screamed, grabbed his head, which ached as though a hand had raked right through it. He drew a great breath, looked to the ground far below. Nothing was familiar. He peered up towards the universe, at a clear inky night spattered with stars. He shot up high above the clouds, towards that clarity, towards what he did know, towards A'vean... home. His speed accelerated through the upper atmosphere; ice encased his skin as the prickle of the universe struck through the darkness of space.

He gasped, the cords of his muscles strained, the veins in his neck bulged and his mark near seared the flesh from his face. He was ready to leave this flesh and blood behind, ready to take back his true form, his true place in the universe. Yeqon tucked his wings as tight as he could, cut through the last layer of the Earth like a spear...

Bang

Something thumped Yeqon backwards, sent him tumbling over and over back through the frozen atmosphere, plummeting beneath the clouds. Down, down, down; light dark, light dark; his arms and legs flailed, his wings couldn't take hold. Air wailed in his ears until he finally tumbled forwards and regained control only moments from hitting the ground. Yeqon took a moment to find his centre, to draw feeling back to his arms and legs, to shake out his wings and find his bearings.

"What…what is going on? I don't understand," he said in a shattered voice to no one… as no one was there to hear him. He spun around a dozen times, inspected everything in his line of sight over and over. Nothing seemed familiar, nothing looked right. His skin crawled with dread. He raked his fingers through his hair, plucked at his lips until they bruised. He looked up, the sky was streaked with white and blue, warm and innocuous with a mid-morning sunlight.

How long have I been lost? He wondered.

He ascended towards the outer reaches of the Earth again, screaming insensibly, spittle flying, freezing into droplets as it hit frigid air. He called on his creator.

"I…'el!" Yeqon breached the upper atmosphere again, felt gravity give way and fire take hold. His body set alight. His skin bubbled; his hair melted away as he aimed for the heavens.

Thump

He tumbled backwards once more, exhausted, agony took over, arms and legs flaccid and weak; he fell. Yeqon tumbled for miles, limp, defeated, utterly confused until he hit the ground at speed, gouging a crater the length of a hundred wing spans.

All was noise, banging and ringing in his head. All was pain. Every patch of skin that was left stung like poison. Yeqon shut down. He closed his eyes, curled into a ball, and let darkness swallow his pain.

Chapter
Fifteen

Two moons had passed before Yeqon awoke and pulled himself from the crater that had cocooned him. He healed what he could with the strength that he had, but he felt weak. His arms quivered and his legs wobbled. His voice was barely a whisper.

"Thank the Throne." He felt his chromious sword at his side. Somehow it had survived the pummelling he had received by forces he didn't understand. He shook, his body trembled.

"No, I rescind that. I thank myself, for you are not with me, Father."

A waning sun tapped Yeqon's raw, new skin, and he retreated into the shadows of leafy trees lining the shore of the beach he had hit. They were trees he did not recognise, smells that were foreign. Even the ground beneath him felt strange. He waited a time, stared out across a gently lapping ocean, and watched seabirds dip and rise from the water until the sky was a bruise and the night air eased his discomfort.

He walked across a soft sand and sighed with the relief of the cool grains against his skin. Squatting down under a virgin moonlight, he ran his hands over his arms, felt the short fuzz of hair that had regrown upon his head. His stomach growled. His mouth was sore and parched; it was hard to swallow. He splashed sea water across his face, regretting the sting of it immediately.

"Argh!" Yeqon punched the ground; sand flew into his face. He spat it out and yelled again. Breathing heavily, his chest ached and his belly growled more urgently.

"I resent this flesh," he grumbled at the need to feed it. Yet, an irreconcilable fear of losing this mortal life set his muscles into action. Yeqon flexed his wings and alighted the island in the middle of the great Southern Ocean. For another night and another day, he hovered in the clouds above it, staring in silence, trying to make sense of where he was, of what had happened.

Kea? Pathos? Kira? He called when a new moon ascended a clear sky. It struck across the ocean, the silvery reflection mirrored Yeqon's outline and he could see just how alone he was.

Ged'erel? "Where is everyone?" he yelled, chest heaving. No answer, not so much as a whisper, not the faintest of thoughts upon the ether. A lonely figure, he became transfixed by his distorted image in the blackness of the water. There was a vastness of nothing behind him, a desolate and silent world in front. The ocean was flat, its stillness seemed to capture the stagnant, strangling feeling that had wrapped around his heart.

He roused from his stare when clouds dulled the moon and his reflection faded. As though snatched from another world, back into the reality of the present, Yeqon's body demanded his attention from thoughts that were tempting, ideas and feelings too dark to speak aloud.

Hunger forced his hand. He descended towards the shoreline and crossed the breadth of the island. He skimmed deep valleys, passed midlands of grassland, until he found a vast mountain range with the smell of sustenance upon it. Yeqon lowered towards the rumble of a waterfall. His feet set upon verdigris stone that led him into a secluded oasis. He stretched his newly healed body, his joints cracked, his muscles felt strong again. He stepped into a waste deep pool, fed readily by the waterfall. The current sped across his skin, cool, cleansing, renewing as it sloughed away the last of his old flesh. He drank deeply from a smaller, moss-rimmed pool, and plucked a curved yellow fruit from a tree. It was soft and sweet, easy to chew where his jaw still ached a little. He rested a time, healed more of his skin with the power that surged strong once more beneath the mortal flesh he endured. He sat again with his heavy thoughts, resting against a vine-clad tree trunk. His eyes were just as heavy, and he let the tension finally release from his limbs. Yeqon shut out the thoughts that tapped at his conscience and allowed the gentle voice of the jungle to soothe him into psynostris, a sleep well needed.

Yeqon hovered again above the island. The full cycle of a day had passed. He had awaited the cover of night and stared across the darkness of a more robust ocean. His mind seemed to cleave in two as he wracked it for memories, for any clue as to where he was. Something blocked access, something robbed him of a part of who he was. His habit of cursing in his native A'vean tongue was the greatest of all assaults… he could not remember; he was unable to recall the words of his own language.

The calm of his rest fell away, and his teeth ground anew. The quietude he had afforded his body was replaced by clenched fists, and a raging ache that clawed through his head. As his breaths raced, his attention fell upon the dawn of the other side of Earth. It struck a thin orange line across the horizon. Something pulled him in that direction, the feeling familiar, but not enough that he actually knew where he was. His fingers tapped his mark as he squinted, head cocked, willing thoughts to come forth. He could almost taste the answers he sought, but something was blocking his memories like a hand slapped across his eyes. He just couldn't see what was plainly in front of him.

Asbel? Ged'erel? He called for help once more. Even his thoughts felt whispered, defeated. Silence answered again. *Koi?* Silence *Kea?* The quiet was so very deafening he pressed his hands against his ears to ease the pain of it.

The entire world felt on a knife's edge. It seemed to be holding its breath. He looked to the stars, sweat broke across his forehead.

"What have you done?" Yeqon's voice was thin; he felt defeated. He coughed, wished he'd taken in more water.

"I'el?" His question cracked. "Please answer me?"

"I'el?" His demand was stronger.

"I'el?" His scream boomed upon the night's breeze, frightened bats from the jungle far below and split his still-dry lips until they bled. He licked blood from the corners of his mouth. The tang of it reminded him of the smell of death, of war, and that was familiar; so, he licked it again.

Yeqon's mortal heart hammered uncomfortably. He rubbed his hand across his chest, felt the breath in his lungs rush too fast; his body trembled. He shook his head, tears burned hot across his new skin. He couldn't look at this strange landscape any longer, he couldn't stand the feeling of loneliness... it was engulfing him.

Yeqon flew for hours, disoriented, trying to remember something, anything, but his mind felt addled, as though unstuffed and re-stuffed with nothing but air. All that was familiar was anger, the sound of flesh peeling apart under the slice of a blade, the way eyes rolled back in a head when death visited. He held onto that.

Beyond the horizon where night met day, something finally *smelled* familiar. He turned sharply towards it; dark thoughts quelled a moment as hope settled into its place. He cautiously descended closer to the ground, where the air was warm and the horizon piqued something in the back of his mind.

Rock-strewn hills, craggy and sharp, lined a blackened landscape. Naked, charred trees bearded the horizon, and immediately below him, the ground was a barren panorama of destruction. No sign of humans anywhere. No sign of his kindred. His heart fluttered once more, a heady mix of panic for his own well-being and deep satisfaction that the smell of humanity wasn't on each breath he drew.

Whatever had occurred, the reason for his pain, confusion and disarray, he knew in his bones that it was because of humans.

Yeqon landed, bare feet sinking into soft, sooty ground. Eyes wide, he called in his mind once more for his kindred as he headed for no particular reason towards a large, sandy mound.

Kea? Kira? Ged'erel?

His feet sunk deeper into the burnt ground as he climbed the mound, still hot, some areas still smouldering. He sniffed; nostrils wide as he drew deeply into his lungs. Something was familiar in the air, a taste, an odour; it made his skin tingle. He rounded the mound until his foot hit something.

He kicked at it with his toes, squatted and dug the sand away.

"I'el!" Yeqon's teeth ground, his breaths quickened again. His hands worked quicker; the skin of his skull seemed to tighten. He scooped his find into his hand, his mouth dropped open.

The gentle light of his mark struck through a diamond skull, shimmering, setting a rainbow spectrum across the mortal remains of a Watcher.

"I don't understand," he whispered. Yeqon shook his head, thoughts cluttered once more. He raked his hands through the sand faster, revealing not one, but two Watcher skeletons entwined. A third lay underneath, human bones cocooned within the gentle hug of the diamond ones.

"No!"

Yeqon dug more chaotically, sweat dripped from his chin as he found another and another A'vean skeleton. Most harboured human remains in their grasp. He slumped onto his backside, wiped a hand across his sweaty face, his eyes stung with misery.

His lower lip quivered. "Kea?" Yeqon whispered.

No, it's not me Yeqon. Kea's voice travelled along the ether.

Yeqon startled. He shot up, spun around, eyes wide, heart hammering. "Where are you?"

Kea appeared before him. Paler than before, hollow under her eyes, she was too thin, her arms and legs crusted with thickened burn scars.

Yeqon flung himself at her. Their fingers dug into each other's skin; their wings cocooned them from the world. They embraced for a day and a night, their energy healing each other, both inside and out. No words were shared until the rise of a new moon.

They sat at the foot of what had been an ancient cypress tree that had guarded the entrance to the underground homes of the Watchers. Leaning against its charred stump, they sat for another full day in silence, staring at A'vean and human remains, trying to make sense of what had occurred.

"I didn't know we could die here," Kea whispered.

Yeqon pondered her comment, picking hardened mud from between his toes.

"We can in physical form. There have been accidents, but our soul returns home to A'vean if that happens." He drew a long breath and looked to the constellations above. "Where have *they* gone?"

"Perhaps they made it out?" Kea said, running a finger along a diamond foot bone.

Yeqon shook his head. "Did you not see them? Their panic? They looked trapped."

Kea sighed, rested her hand upon his shoulder. "It was chaos. I'm not sure what I saw, Yeqon."

"It seems to me that they were caught as unaware as we were." Yeqon glanced at Kea, his eyes still red-rimmed. "Where have they gone if they did not leave the Earth?"

"Perhaps they found another way?" Kea suggested, then frowned. "For some reason though, I can't seem to recall where that could be. I feel a little strange. My thoughts are..."

Yeqon shrugged her hand from his shoulder. His head hung low whilst his finger traced a circle over and over in the soot he sat upon.

"Something catastrophic has occurred. I can feel the presence of many A'vean souls." He looked behind, then back to the sky. "Can't you feel their sorrow? They're lost, looking for somewhere safe on this forsaken hole of a rock." Yeqon kicked out at the ground, blackened dirt sprayed back, caught upon the night breeze.

Kea coughed it away, sniffed, and reached for the diamond bones they had kept company. Her fingers twitched away quickly, as though the bones stung. She drew her knees up and leaned her head on them. She sighed, her attention weary and heavy upon the remains.

"They tried to shield the humans, but His power, I'el's anger, it was just too strong," she said.

Yeqon's circling had ceased, and he stared at the bones, reached forward and touched one, pulling back just as Kea had.

"We are shamed, Yeqon. Banished, punished most severely," Kea said. Her eyes flicked to the stars. "And we all suffer now for it." Her hand slid back to the bones; she forced the touch despite the tremor of her fingers. A silvery tear slipped down her face.

"Shamed? Banished? For what?" Yeqon watched her gently trail the bone of the unknown Watcher.

"For what we did. Don't you remember?" Kea asked, sympathetic eyes scanning his scars; she reached for his face. "Your hair, it's darker." She traced her finger along a lock of his hair. "Perhaps it's the shock?"

Yeqon shook his head, yanking his hair from her touch. He clasped his hands around his temples, his fingers dug into his scalp.

"I… we were feasting, the Eloi were giving me grief for enjoying humans too much but…" His eyes widened; his mouth gaped. "It was…"

"The cry of that baby. It sealed our fate, Yeqon." Kea sniffed, lashes shimmering.

Yeqon's fingers curled harder into his hair as flashes of memory flooded his mind. The human woman, the blood, the child… a Nephilim, and the Arc Angels setting the world alight.

"*Our* fate? *I* did not breed with a human!" Yeqon snapped. "Why should I suffer for the actions of others?"

"You're not alone, my friend." Kea reached for Yeqon again; he yanked his hand away.

"Don't!"

"I'm sorry, Yeqon." She edged away, respecting his sorrow.

They sat in silence a while longer. The rising night's breeze sucked sand along the ground. It curled away from them, growing stronger until a dust devil danced its way towards a clutch of skeletal trees in the distance.

"Where is everyone else?" Yeqon asked, watching the dust devil collapse into nothingness as the wind gave up. He swallowed hard. It seemed his very existence was the same as that dust devil.

"Scattered. Confused," Kea answered. "Ged'erel is looking for you, as is Asbel. I asked them to stay with me, but they're frightened, angry; it's understandable."

She watched Yeqon, who stared, unblinking, at the ground.

"Perhaps some escaped home just in time. Perhaps some are hiding with Asbel and Ged'erel? I imagine, many more might..." Kea stopped, her eyes lingered on the diamond skeleton.

Yeqon sucked in a sharp breath, his attention locked on the same remains as well.

Do I know you? He stared deeply into the shine of the bone.

As he wracked his mind for the familiarity of it, his fingers found the pocket he'd stuffed the soul in days ago. Despite what he'd been through, the chromious lined belt and pocket had survived, along with his battle-ready sword. The soul was still there, wriggling frantically against his hip. His eyes flicked to the sky, then back to the bones. His fingers cupped the pocket as though that soul was the most precious thing he had left.

"Kira?" Yeqon asked, his eyes finding Kea's.

Kea sobbed, "That's not her." She swallowed hard; the renewed shimmer in her lashes fell down her cheeks. "I've searched everywhere for her." She pulled a small object from her pocket, fingers uncurling, a diamond finger bone shone in her palm. "This is all I could find."

"She's gone?" Yeqon's voice ripened with rage.

Kea's fingers curled protectively back over the bone. She looked at her hands, turned them over, inspecting them. "I had hold of her for as long as I could. I did, I really did try, but…"

Yeqon reached for Kea's hands, drew them into his.

"This is *not* your fault, Kea." His voice shook, "This is His fault." He glared at the sky.

Kea sniffed, shook her head. "No, it's not I'el's fault. It's on us… well, not me, I suppose. I just arrived, but those of us who didn't obey His rules; they put this into motion. Everyone was accountable for knowing what was going on and not putting a stop to it."

Kea winced as Yeqon's hands curled tighter around hers. "You can't possibly convince yourself of that?" His eyes bored at her until she looked up, and she was hooked by their depth and a darkness circling his irises. Yeqon's grip eased and his thumbs swept over the back of her hands.

"Kea, we've interfered, interjected, and annihilated other species across the universes where we saw fit for the betterment of nature. Why has that been acceptable, yet the most minor of fraternisation here has *us* almost annihilated? And for what? A creature that couldn't drag itself from the swamps or the trees without our power in the first place? It's hypocrisy!"

"*Give them a little spark… oh, but not too much… wait a minute, give them a little more… but no, don't enjoy anything… hang on, hide in the shadows and watch them fall over themselves making the most imbecilic of decisions…*" Yeqon mocked the ancient directive they'd been tasked with.

"Stop!" Kea said. "I know it doesn't make sense. What He wants of this planet has never been completely clear. I don't understand it either, but I don't need to. Everything is done for His supreme design of the universes. Only I'el understands the intricacies of that. He keeps the universes in harmony because of His will, because He created it all. We have to trust in I'el… as awful as this is, as hard as it is… whatever it is."

Yeqon released her hands, pushing them away. He stood, bent to the left, then the right, and cracked every bone in his spine.

"No! It's not right, Kea. *We* are superior, we offer our strength and our benevolence, we offer our power and compassion, but this is *too* far. Humanity is no more precious than any other. In fact, they are the weakest species I've had the misfortune to come across. There is *nothing* redeeming about them at all. They would have died out long ago if not for us. They are feeble, wicked, and stupid. Greater civilisations have come before them that deserved us. I *won't* suffer because of them." Yeqon's body was rigid, his wings released, one hand over the soul, his other hand drummed against his Mark of A'vean.

"Yeqon…"

"I'll not help another human; I'll not suffer another moment hiding. I'll not put *my* wellbeing at risk for a single one of them."

"Yeqon stop this!" Kea stood, rounded on him. "If we are stuck here, if... I think we are stuck here…" She rubbed her temples, trying to jog her memories. "I don't know about you, but my memories are not right. I can't remember our language, everything is… not right. Whatever has happened, we have to stick together now, take care of each other, pull the pieces of this planet back together until I'el forgives us. Humanity has suffered too, and it isn't their fault. Many of them have been wiped out, most in fact from what I've seen. The planet has burned. We should help those we can, show I'el we can and will set humans back on track and under their own evolutionary road."

Yeqon stared at Kea. His face tightened; his teeth bared. "No!"

Yeqon walked away. "I'll find a way out; I'll not suffer another moment with this fetid ground under my feet." He walked faster, then he ran until his legs burned… and finally he flew. Kea screamed in his mind; he ignored her. Yeqon flew low, took in the landscapes rushing fast beneath him. Carnage was definitely there. Death hung in the air; it scorched the earth, the taste of it coated his throat. He closed his eyes, searched his memories for something, for anything. The ancient stone henge of the north came to mind, and he transferred.

Chapter Sixteen

Frigid wind sucked Yeqon out of the ether. His feet sunk into icy mud. He was met with a scene not unlike the last days of Satanos. Bodies were strewn across the landscape. Burnt corpses, some to bone, some to ash, some still held onto flesh that dripped with rot and maggots. Ravens feasted, vermin scattering with their scraps. Yeqon kicked through it all, no care for a skull that rolled from its neck, no sorrow for the ones melted together in death.

The henge was a mess, half collapsed, its light doused, its power to transport him away clipped, just like Göbekli Tepe. He knew there were others, but no matter how hard he concentrated, he couldn't recall where the other portals were.

"Damn you!" he yelled, but this time, did not afford I'el his attention for more than a moment. He spat on the ground, stood on the phlegm, imagined it to be his creator. The feeling flushed his skin, a strange pleasure not felt before, and he fanned that feeling. Yeqon coveted it. It doused the pain; it hid the torment.

He made his way to the altar stone, hand on the soul, mind still cluttered, rage pulsing hot under his skin. Anger felt better, anger felt powerful. It seemed to be the only power present. The energy of the henge had faded, the buzz of it a memory. A few days ago, its power would make his skin tingle, the hum of it audible a day's flight away. But now…

Yeqon sat upon the altar stone and looked at the great blue pillars. He squeezed his eyes, his vision a little hazy. The henge faded in and out of focus.

Where am I? He massaged his temples, the soul ever agitated by his side, a growing pain in his eyes now excruciating. He stared at the surrounds, a frown creasing his face. He couldn't quite remember what he was doing or what this place of ruins was.

"Argh!" He bent over, scooped snow from the mud, and pressed it against his eyelids.

"What is happening?" he asked no one but himself.

As the pain ebbed, he blinked the snow away, rubbed his eyes clear and stared anew at his surrounds.

Yeqon frowned again; his mouth opened a crack. He stood, turned slowly, one hand on the soul, the other plucked at his beard. He felt as though he had awoken from sleep.

"Where am I?" he muttered.

"What is this place?" Yeqon spun to find Kea staring at the surrounds just like he was. "You're easy to track. All that anger leaves a hot trail." She followed Yeqon about the henge. "Looks old. Do you know what it is? Why did you come here?" Kea trailed her fingers over the stones, her eyes vacant. "There's something about this place."

"I don't know what… no... I can't..." He tapped his head with his palm. "I was with you, then found myself here after an ache nearly blinded me." Yeqon threaded around the still-standing stones, Kea in tow. He rubbed his eyes, both now swollen. "I feel like I should know where I am."

A wind picked up; it held the cool taste of rain. The sky darkened, clouds blew in fast, hail soon followed.

Fat rain drops belted their skin; the wind whipped hard; the hail bruising. The air rang with the sound of a transfer. Yeqon and Kea turned, eyes shielded with their hands.

"Asbel!" Yeqon drew him in. "You're safe."

Asbel shook his head. The honey of his skin had paled, its smoothness marred with healing wounds as well. "Thank I'el. I've been looking for everyone, for someone. I heard you, you're the first I've found since…"

"Since our father betrayed us?" Yeqon snapped. "Don't thank Him for anything."

Asbel stared at Yeqon; his throat bobbed; his eyes narrowed. He limped closer, his left leg thick with large scabs and swellings. "Those Arc Angels. They've destroyed nearly everything."

Yeqon nodded, his knuckles whitened as he curled his fingers around his sword. The soul writhed as though it felt the change coursing through Yeqon's insides. Energy sparked along his arms; his pupils dilated for a fraction of a second before returning to a bloodshot blue hue.

"Well, they haven't destroyed me, Asbel, but they'll wish they had." Yeqon sucked a deep breath through his teeth.

"Yeqon, don't let anger rule…"

"Enough Kea! If you want to grovel at His feet, if you wish to thank I'el for this…" Yeqon stretched his arms wide, sword now heavy in his right hand. He jerked his head towards the dead bodies, pointed the tip at one, flipping a charred skull from left to right.

"Go ahead, Kea. Be my guest." Yeqon weaved through the henge, sword singing along the stones, trying to understand why this place felt familiar, why it felt important. He ran his hand along the flat of his sword, tipped it and did the same along its razored edge until a seam of blood drizzled from thumb to elbow.

Kea winced, Asbel licked his lips, eyes flitting skyward.

"We have been wronged, Asbel. We have been robbed of our freedom, of our…" Yeqon tapped the flat of the sword against his head, squeezed his eyes, trying to force resistant memories forward. "Our memories…" Yeqon thread through the last pillars, picking up the half-burned carcass of a human, and dragged it back towards the altar stone.

"Yeqon… what's going on? What are you doing?" Kea asked.

Asbel's eyes widened. Sweat beaded at his brow as he watched the body bump along behind Yeqon.

"What's going on? I'll tell you exactly what *is* going on, Kea." Yeqon hoisted the corpse onto the altar stone, then he pulled the soul from his pocket. It writhed desperately through his fingers; he bared his teeth at it. "Submit!" he growled. The soul panicked, tried to leap from his grasp.

Kea gasped. "Yeqon!"

"Quiet!" Yeqon bellowed. Kea flinched as darker clouds rolled in, as though magnetised to his anger. Thunder rumbled and lightning blanketed the horizon. Wind blew rain into his eyes, yet they widened and a dark hue returned to the blueness of them.

"I said… submit!" Yeqon hissed at the soul.

The soul in his palm; it quivered and curled obediently into a tiny iridescent coil.

"Yeqon! Stop! That's a..." Kea slapped a hand on her mouth.

"Yes, it is a…" He smiled garishly at the light in his palm "… a human soul, and it will be repayment for what *I* have lost. It will be retribution and deliverance."

Kea's wings expanded; hail hissed through their power, but they glowed brighter. The mark over her right eye fluoresced, and her palms shimmered with power as she reached for a weapon.

"Don't do this, Yeqon!" she said.

Asbel eased back, fingers aglow. One hand hovered above his own sword. He licked his lips, eyes swinging between Kea and Yeqon as though assessing his options.

Thunder raged; the ground slickened with mud. Kea elevated from its sludge and pointed sharply at Yeqon.

"Put… the soul... back!" Kea demanded.

Yeqon closed his fingers over the soul. Kea winced, felt the soul's pain, its fear and abandonment.

"Put it back, Yeqon!" Kea lunged for his hand.

Yeqon's free hand arced across Kea's face. She gasped and fell back into the mud, her cheek split open. Kea recoiled, the air snapped with energy around her, her hand alight with an orb. She rose again.

Asbel drew his sword, edged closer to Yeqon.

"I'll not warn you again. Put the soul back, Yeqon," Kea demanded, jerking her head sharply to flick blood from her face.

Yeqon smiled, his teeth bared. "Put it back? Very well, Kea." Yeqon's arm wound back, Kea screamed, and released her orb. The orb flew towards Yeqon, the air sung with its buzz, aimed directly for his heart until Asbel's sword cut through its flight path. The orb extinguished. Kea gasped, stared in shock at Asbel who alighted the ground, his face a mix of shock and delight. He pumped his wings once, swung around and kicked Kea in the chest. Kea spun backwards, hit the ground hard, gasping, unused to her new mortal flesh in battle.

Yeqon smiled more deeply and nodded at Asbel. He reached towards the altar stone, towards the human corpse. He yanked it up by a tuff of remaining hair and rammed the soul down its throat.

The corpse thudded back to the ground. Yeqon wiped his hands together.

The storm stopped dead; the rain ceased. Quiet tightened its grip on the Earth.

"Oh …Yeqon! What have you done?" Kea stumbled back to her feet, dazed, winded, blood still running down her cheek.

"You asked me to put it back, Kea, and that I have." Yeqon reached back down and shook the corpse. "Come on, don't make me wait!"

The corpse's bony fingers twitched, its sinewy skull shifted, the teeth clacking together. Decaying limbs jerked; the body rolled over. Gurgling sounds filled the heavy silence as it pulled itself to its feet.

All three watched the dead reanimate.

"This is everything nature did not intend. You will suffer for this." Kea wiped blood from her face with the back of her hand and backed away as Yeqon pointed at the corpse.

"Handsome rogue, aren't you? Come here," Yeqon ordered.

Asbel edged closer, watching the corpse find its balance, its bones cracking, sinews snapping as it took two awkward steps towards Yeqon.

"Now my little Rogue, pull your arm off," Yeqon commanded. Kea backed away until she hit the outer edge of the henge. Asbel watched with wide-eyed delight.

The Rogue reached its right arm to its left. It threaded its finger bones through the arm bone and tugged. It pulled, it gurgled and snapped, then wobbled on its feet until the arm was pulled clean from the socket.

"You told me not to let anger rule, Kea. Anger is not what I feel, it is not what I desire." Yeqon smiled at the Rogue. "Sit."

The Rogue flopped to the ground at his feet.

"Until I'el is obliterated, until the Throne of A'vean falls, *vengeance* will be my will, *vengeance* will rule my every action." Yeqon's hands lit white. He thrust them skyward and released pulses of energy.

Thunder clapped anew, lightning struck close, a tree exploded in the nearby forest. Yeqon mounted the altar stone.

"Vengeance will flood this world," he bellowed as he waved his hands over his head. Clouds shimmered; their colour deepened to a sickening green. A great aperture appeared above as Yeqon continued pulsing the sky.

"You can join me, Kea, or be my enemy, for no servant of I'el shall walk in peace by my side." The wind built, it swirled faster, Asbel looked up. Adoration drew a deeper colour to his face.

"I will follow you," Asbel said, and he mounted the altar stone by Yeqon's side. The one-armed Rogue corpse wobbled at their feet.

Yeqon pushed him down. "Go then, Asbel, find us the like-minded, bring them to me and we shall rain fire upon this world like no Arc Angel ever has! Humans will bear my wrath and not have peace until I am avenged of this injustice. I will deliver them all that they desire and rob them of it at the same time."

Asbel's face lit. He stretched his wings wide, bowed before Yeqon, and disappeared in a flash of light.

The aperture in the clouds stretched wider, a stink eked from it that made Kea gag. She stumbled further away. Yeqon peered up into the mouth of his creation. A strange sun bore its heat upon him and he breathed deep. Thunder boomed from this new realm.

"Kea?"

"Go to Hell, Yeqon!"

He laughed, "I am Hell, and now I will drag this entire world there with me."

Yeqon stretched his wings wide, his mark glimmered, its coloured deepened from silver to black. His wings faded from pearlescent to a murky grey. As he stood upon the altar stone of the northern henge, buffeted by a rising storm, his hair blackened and his pupils dilated until light no longer shone from within. The pure power of A'vean blue relinquished to demonic darkness.

The first Satan was born.

The End

135

Keep reading…

Awaken *book 1*

Prologue and Chapter One

Prologue

12,000 years ago

As charcoal clouds mustered on the horizon, the sun still shone bright and warm from behind the billowing mass. With sleek, muscled arms, Nik'ael gripped at an overhanging branch leaning out from the shade, plucked a hard, green olive, and inspected it. Perfect! Beads of sweat glistened at his temples; the heat of summer was at its peak. A white linen chiton kept him cool as it flapped in the breeze against his thighs. He let go of the branch and unclasped his water pouch from the woven belt strung loosely around his hips. He drew a long, refreshing gulp. The rolling clouds mirrored across his sparkling blue eyes as he caught sight of his reflection in the silver clasp, reminding him all too well of what he was. He smiled as his alabaster hair blew around his square jaw as an emerging breeze rustled the leaves above his head.

A storm was brewing; he would have to cut short his walk today. He enjoyed his long walks where he surveyed his crops and rested his mind amongst the peaceful quiet of the orchard. He smiled broadly to himself, deepening the dimples on his golden cheeks. The harvest was plentiful-they would all eat heartily this year. A rumble of thunder in the distance set him on his way down the grassy hill towards home. He rolled the unripened olive between his finger and thumb as he went.

Nik'ael surveyed expansive plains as he descended from the rise of the hilltop. This is a paradise on Earth, he thought. He contemplated the small village that was his home—a collective of family and friends who lived and worked in harmony. It was an eclectic mix of people who laughed and loved, regardless of who or what they were. Illness was rare, lives were long, and the land upon which he stood sustained them well. Nik'ael looked skyward and wondered why, even now, he and his kindred were still unable to visit their true homeland, despite all their good works for the human population.

Many years had come to pass since life was breathed into the first soul in this world. Distant thunder rumbled as he took in the parched surrounds, and he thought about his ancestors who had been sent to watch over this new mortal species called humans, both a blessing and a curse. For, once on Earth, these Watchers of the Kingdom of A'vean succumbed to the impulses of the human condition, breaking the law of the Kingdom. They discovered urges of the flesh that they had hitherto never known, and fell in love and lusted after these weak but beautiful beings, creating offspring such as he, Nik'ael, son of Toth'iel.

These offending Watchers were sent to Earth to oversee and protect humans, nothing more. Breeding with them was considered heinous by the Throne, a great betrayal of the innocence of humankind.

The Watchers were banished without recourse to live amongst humankind, forever unable to return home. New afflictions beset the Watchers, no doubt punishment for their weakness. Bitterness and anger brewed within them, a new scourge which they suffered in the human form, and which divided them into factions. Nik'ael was one of the Eudaimonia—the Flourishing Ones—hybrids who had merged through necessity into a peaceful life on Earth among the humans. They continued to teach and care for man whilst learning from their ancestors' painful experience to no longer mix their progenitors' bloodline with mortals.

Realising the damage they had caused, many of the offending Watchers had largely removed themselves from contact with humans, preferring to retreat within the shadows into a hidden life. A select few stayed to guide their Eudaimonian offspring in the ways of the ancestors in the Secret Places hidden throughout the world. They protected the descendants from themselves and their enemies.

As strong as Nik'ael was, even he feared the others, those in exile who became The Daimon—vengeful Watchers who had vowed to rise against A'vean. Reviled by their predicament, they disappeared, not heard from for centuries, but remained ever-present, ominous and unseen.

As Nik'ael travelled home, leaving behind him the olive trees he loved so much, something touched him lightly upon his shoulder. He turned, and his eyes widened in surprise for a moment. In his three hundred years, he had never seen such a being. Uriel, an Archangel from the High Council of A'vean towered over him.

Nik'ael bowed deeply, eyes cast down.

"Stand, young Nik'ael, I wish you no harm. I wish only to speak with you."

"Kindred, you have my ear and my heart, but I cannot stand in your presence," he quietly responded as he laid his arm upon his bent knee.

"Many years have passed since we could consider ourselves kindred, Nik'ael, yet I bring you a warning at the peril of my divine soul. You are descended of my brother Toth'iel who sinned along with the others. I have watched with regret his fate and that of his lineage. Entrenched in the mortal realm eternally is truly horrendous," he shook his head in despair. "You, Nik'ael, have lived with dignity amongst humankind and have not followed in your father's way."

Nik'ael cringed inwardly at the insult. His father had been a great warrior who had made one simple mistake. He was too scared to share these feelings. He did not know the temperament of an Archangel first-hand to dare to contradict one.

Uriel continued. "I have heard your confessions of remorse for the sins of your forebears. Your undertakings to be of service to the Throne in protecting man and woman from further degradation have not gone unnoticed."

Nik'ael attempted to speak, but Uriel struck him silent with the wave of his hand.

"For this reason, I grant you a small mercy. I am here on the orders of the Throne, directly from the great I'el, to warn our humble servant Noah of a great flood. It shall deluge the Earth catastrophically, so as to purge all of the evil from this once beautiful creation. Take refuge Nik'ael. Warn your worthy kindred, for I pity your poor souls."

Nik'ael was silent for a moment, his mouth hung slightly open in shock. He looked upwards, barely daring to meet the eyes of Uriel. Surely this could not be? His Creators were not vengeful. Were they not benevolent, especially to those who shared the spirit and power of A'vean running through their veins? His mind raced for answers.

Uriel rose into the sky as glaring white light and heat emanated from behind him. His eyes swirled like supernovas, a mishmash of coloured, sparkling light. In a booming voice he called out, "You have been warned. Dismiss me at your peril."

He was gone in a blinding flash that left Nik'ael reeling from the aftershock, thrust back onto the ground with the breath knocked from his lungs. As he recovered from the encounter, he drew himself up and fled.

Despite a superhuman speed, he worried that his mortal legs would not get him home fast enough to warn his village. Against all his instincts, he forced himself to stop, close his eyes and relax his mind. Connecting with the elements, he drew in the energy surging on the breeze, and rose up into the sky just as Uriel had. Nik'ael felt the ripples of energy surging from within-an instinct he had suppressed more often than not. Doubt plagued him as his back burned and his muscles flexed. He could never match the power of an Archangel yet he knew he possessed an immense strength which was unusual for a hybrid. He comforted his confidence with this thought as he let himself relax. Nik'ael flew upon the cooling breeze, through the ever-darkening sky.

The ground flew by below, but not nearly fast enough in this moment of desperation. He quietly cursed himself for not practicing his higher abilities more often. He never really needed to. By the time he reached the valley where he lived, an ominous and heavy rain was drenching the landscape.

Nik'ael called out frantically to his family as a feeling of doom suddenly overwhelmed him. Neither human, Eudaimonian, nor Watcher responded. The bang of a door against a nearby house set him on edge as the breeze screeched wildly through the village, like the howls of a Daimon in the pits of Hell. Distressed chickens clucked and squawked as they dashed for cover. A cow had pulled itself free from its tether and seemed disorientated, nosing through barrels of grain, the whites of its eyes bulging.

Searching every home and field, he found nothing but signs of hasty retreat. The rain pelted his body. In the distance, through the hideous sounds of the angry storm, he thought he heard a scream. He felt fear and pain, but not his own. Drawing as much energy as he could, he crested the rocky hill that protected his village from the ocean winds, only to be confronted by a scene of utter horror.

There, upon the beach and bathed in a blinding light, were his family and friends being slaughtered by High Angels. Humans were being thrown like sacks, smashing their brittle bodies into barely recognisable remnants. The odour of blood made his stomach lurch with nausea. The unnatural redness running into the sea foam was hard to watch, yet he could not look away. Watchers and Eudaimonians had their spines ripped out rendering them unable to commune with the elements. Fresh muscle and bone littered the sand, leaving them vulnerable and paralysed, unable to save themselves through flight or transference. The dark blood of the Watchers and the crimson of the humans, congealed into pools of horror before it was lapped up by the incoming tide. Nik'ael hid behind a large rock, watching the bloody murder with disbelieving eyes. He was frozen in place. He could not have moved from his hiding spot even if he'd wanted to.

As though time stood still, this scene seemed to last forever — like it was occurring in the slow motion of a nightmare. The paralysis of shock numbed him, and his body was immovable from the ground.

When all of the humans were dead and the Earth-bound Watchers were rendered completely defenceless and unconscious, the avenging Angels ascended up to the clouds and disappeared, their mission complete.

Torrential rain fell with a deafening roar. Nik'ael's hair was plastered to his face. His tears and the hammering droplets of rain were indistinguishable now. Shock had heightened his senses, every hair on his body stood frozen, every cell intimately aware of the suffering below. Pain shot through him as though he himself was under attack. His stomach heaved at the metallic odour of the inconceivable torrents of thick, glistening blood as it drained from the sand into the ever-encroaching tide. What was once pristine white, was now stained a dark, sickening red.

Nik'ael slowly rose out of his hiding place, shamed by his cowardice. Uriel warned me too late, he thought to himself. They had no chance at all. Was that his intention? Was he being fooled by design? Was he to be punished by bearing witness to such carnage?

Still in shock, he made his way unsteadily by foot down to the beach. Stepping through the masses of bloodied bodies, he kneeled by a human companion, a young man so broken from within that he was now a mere sack of skin. Lifeless eyes looked up at him. Poor Evane—such a kind soul. He scanned the beach, short of breath from the sorrow as he found himself surrounded by hundreds of lifeless and dying corpses, most of whom he knew. The wind blew hard into him, whipping at him from all directions. The sea spray burned his eyes and the sand bit hard at his skin as he searched on. He was unable to heal the mortal wounds of his kindred by himself—there were too many—and the poor humans had no hope at all.

Furthest away from the menacing tide, high up on the beach, he came upon a figure whose familiarity brought him to his knees instantly. Lying atop a small rise of craggy shoreline rock, a female lay prone. Her back was flayed wide open, her beautiful earthly body completely ruined. Nik'ael crawled to her on hand and knee—such was the effect that the sight had upon him. He reached out to her still warm but ghastly pale flesh and rolled her over into his lap. He knew who she was even before he saw her beautiful face. He could tell by the curve of her body, the impossibly long plaited white locks, now bloodstained and cascading down her lithe physique. Across his lap, mortally wounded and limp as a rag, was his wife, Neren'iel. Her soul was no longer with him. As a half-breed, she was unable to withstand the immense power of an avenging Angel, and these wounds could not be healed. He gently picked up her hands and kissed her fingers, already tinged blue by the touch of death. He wanted to die right then and there with her. Pulling her up higher into his lap, he cried out, his head thrown back in anguish. Hot tears cascaded down his face, mirroring the rain pounding upon his back. The physical droplets of his grief diluted the blood that encrusted her angelic face. He could not feel her energy any longer. He could not feel anything at all.

After a time, Nik'ael was forced to carefully lay her back upon the ground. A soft and lingering kiss was placed upon her lips, a whisper of eternal love promised into her unhearing ears. He ran his hand one last time down the length of her hair, caressing her soft, pale skin under his trembling hand, embedding her visage and feel into his memory. He rose into the sky, weakened by what he had seen on the ground. The ocean was rising and raging at an incredible speed. Tsunami-like waves crashed further and down deeper onto the peninsula, engulfing everything in sight. Were any of his kind able to survive this? He turned his back, no longer able to look. In the distance, he saw her—she was fleeing over the farmland. Had she sat there like him and done nothing, too? He closed his eyes. He was utterly alone, deserted, betrayed.

Nik'ael flew for what felt like an eternity, his own tears adding to the steadily filling oceans. The sky overhead was smudged crystalline by the icy comet that had exploded above the earth, now raining its remnants down. He found small ports of rest on the peaks of the highest hills and mountains not yet engulfed by A'vean's wrath. Nothing made sense. I'el was peace, A'vean the ultimate place of oneness, or so he had been taught as a child. His confusion slowly turned to the beginnings of anger.

Finally, he spotted out at sea a vessel of such magnitude that he thought for a moment that he was hallucinating. His body was weak and ravaged. Following the ship's path for a time through the roiling waters, he finally flew down and rapped on its doors.

An oaken porthole opened on the side and an aged fellow thrust his head out, looking about for the disturbance. The wind and sea spray blew savagely into his greying hair and beard.

He glared in surprise at Nik'ael, who cried out to him, "Noah, beloved of The Most High of A'vean, please will you offer me sanctuary? I was warned too late by the Archangel Uriel, of this horrific tragedy. I've witnessed my family slaughtered. I am lost." The human weakness deep within him surfaced as he begged for help.

Noah looked at him momentarily then wordlessly shut the window.

Shock, abandonment, utter misery, and loneliness assaulted Nik'ael's senses.

He clenched his eyes and fists, his mouth thin with building rage. All the muscles of his body rippled beneath his golden skin. Tossed around in the sky by the cyclonic winds, he threw back his head and let out a scream so primal, so loud and reverberating, that it penetrated every corner of the Earth. His veins strained against his skin through this outpouring of passion. The swirling mark upon his face lit up like a beacon, blazing across the waters below. Something snapped within him. When his energy was finally depleted, he quieted. Nik'ael opened his eyes wide and clear. He looked back up to the furthest reaches of the sky and spoke with an unnerving calm.

"I will have my revenge against you. A worthy servant was I to you and of all those seated by your table. You reward me, a victim of circumstance, with such betrayal? I curse all that follow the Throne of A'vean, and I vow to cause chaos and harm for the rest of my days."

Nik'ael drifted silently through the air, his head low in defeat. Through bloodshot eyes, he glared at his reflection in the glassy water below. Angry tears worked their way slowly over his flaring nostrils, then languidly dripped from the edge of his locked jawline. His shadow and reflection suddenly disappeared as the dull sunlight was blotted out behind him. He spun around, still dominated by fear, and his hands flung back in defence. There before him hovered five malevolent figures. Instinctively he knew them.

Yeqon, Ged'erel, Asbel, Pineme, and Kasadya. The Five Satans, forever present but always unseen.

Yeqon moved forward and spoke. "Brother, we heard your grief from every realm. We are one and the same. Take my hand. Join us. Together, our power combined, we shall avenge all that have wronged us."

Without hesitation, and in a moment of pure weakness, Nik'ael reached out and grabbed Yeqon's hand.

A powerful, dark energy shot through Nik'ael, piercing every cell in a nanosecond of pure agony. His eyes turned from blue opals to black, and his heart went from feeling, to stone cold.

Nik'ael was now the sixth Satan.

I always knew I was different. Not weird or quirky, just different... well maybe a little weird, but weird is completely okay. I look just like everyone else my age, mostly. On a deeper level though, I knew that what made me human was more ethereal than I was comfortable admitting, even to myself. Snippets of my abilities had been shining through my entire life. What I thought I was, and the truth of its meaning, were about to bring me crashing down into a level of chaos I could have never imagined.

Chapter

One

Cockatoos screeched like washerwomen shouting orders for the day as I emerged from the fog of sleep. A blaring alarm, getting louder by each ignored minute, nearly imploded the iPhone by the bedside. Finally, I slipped my hand from under the duvet, touched the dismiss button, then flung the whole device across the room.

Refusing to open my eyes, I slithered from bed. In a well-practiced routine, I made my way to the bathroom by feel alone. Flipping the light switch on, glare reflected in the mirror, forcing wakefulness upon me.

"Ugh!" Who invented mornings? Were they thinking straight?

Turning worn brass faucets on, I waited for the shower to heat up. The gentle spray of water on the curtain and rising steam beckoned. I stepped in, leaned against the wall and relaxed.

Shift work. The early starts and night shifts were the pits, but it's what I did, because I loved my job. Nursing rewarded that selfish part of me that liked the indulgence of making a difference, of saving a life, and knowing that it was my actions that did it. I would have preferred it though if people could choose their moments of sickness to occur in more socially acceptable hours.

Healing came naturally to me from my earliest memories. Anyone I saw in pain — be it a person or a poor creature found on the side of the road — I had to care for them. A legacy bestowed by my family. Generations of healers, seers, mystics, you name it. Everyone, according to Nan, experienced something different as their gift. We could probably open up a sideshow at a carnival, except that our powers were more than a money-gouging stunt. They were organic and real, but hidden. On the hospital wards, I could gently and discreetly unfurl small amounts of my secret gift as it developed. A nursing career allowed me the freedom to be me, Sophia Woodville, without standing out too much.

After a few minutes, feeling slightly more human, I stepped out. Lavender moisturiser melted into my still-warm skin. I swiped the steam from the mirror and slid in my contacts. Warm brown eyes reflected back. I slathered on some foundation, a sweep of mascara, and aloe lip balm. A touch of makeup was necessary whenever I left the house, just enough to cover the large swirling tendrils of the birth mark that covered my right eye and cheek. I'd never been ashamed of it, but the veil of light beige saved strangers from staring or voicing the odd, awkward question. It wasn't a particularly bad birthmark. In fact, Nan instilled in me that it was beautiful; another part of my heritage.

My ordinary, covered up reflection stared back. I saved a little rebellion for my hair — I wasn't a complete bore. Rainbow tinted tresses slid through my brush as I wound hues of pale blue, pink, and green into a messy bun. I smiled. It reminded me of my rotation in paediatrics. A nurse who looked like a fairy broke down all the scary barriers that kids hid behind. It was an icebreaker and a crowd pleaser, especially if you were five years old. I thought Nan's proper old-world ways would object, but she was surprisingly modern by suggesting that it looked enchanting.

Back in my sunlit room, I threw on aqua scrubs and a worn pair of running shoes. Dropping to the floor, I fished under the bed for my ID lanyard when it occurred to me that I hadn't received my regular, silence-shattering 5:45am wakeup call from my bestie, Jasmine. Then I remembered why when I caught sight of the smashed phone in the corner, resting on the ever-growing pile of crumbled clothes.

Crap, another one. Annoyed, I grabbed it off a red top, finding my ID underneath. That's the third time I'd assaulted an innocent phone to death this year. I offset this aggression with the fact I didn't do it to living things. It was becoming a costly character fault though.

I rummaged around on my bedside table, looking for the landline under a pile of books, when my door creaked open. Within seconds, I was flung to the ground by a mass of black and white fur.

"Shadow, you smelly old thing, no morning breath kisses!" Plastered to the floor, I snuggled my Alaskan malamute and constant shadow, hence the name. I wriggled out from under his sloppy, love-struck licking and pointed to the bed.

"Go on now, back to bed." All seventy kilograms of dog heaved up onto the bed. He snapped the quilt in his mouth and pulled it up over himself, resting his head ceremoniously upon the pillow. I giggled, thinking I should've YouTubed that.

Dusting off his fluff from my scrubs, I dialled Jasmine's number.

"Hey you, what's up with voicemail?" she demanded. "Don't tell me you're not coming in today. It's our first day in the ER, and I'm sweating bullets here. I need you as my wingman, or person — or whatever!"

Ride of the Valkyries blared in the background of her phone. Jaz presented herself to the world as a hard-core emo, gothic chick. Her true self was closely guarded, even from me at times. I'd learned never to question her secret stash of classical music.

"Morning Jaz. Calm down, I just murdered another phone!" I confessed. "I'm going to have to pad my walls to protect the next one that succumbs to my morning wrath."

"You're going to be working just to fund new phones," she said. "We've got to work on your morning mood," Jaz laughed, vastly improving my attitude in an instant.

"If you're lucky, I'll pick you up in twenty," then mumbled through my parting goodbye, "Isn't it about time you got a licence?"

Avoiding the third last step with the betraying creak, I snuck downstairs and peeked in on Nan. All was quiet. The purr of the cat was whirring away on the end of her bed. As with every morning, I set out a teapot of English breakfast leaves and a blue willow teacup and saucer. The kettle was filled so that when she woke up, Nan just had to press a button, wait 60 seconds, pour, and enjoy. I slipped a ladybug design tea pot cosy, knitted by Nan, over the pot, grabbed my keys and handbag, knitted by Nan, a slice of sourdough bread, and headed out the door.

The air was cool, the crunch of my steps along the gravel path disturbed a delicate dawn silence. My Mini Cooper started with a welcoming rumble, setting some birds to flight from nearby eucalypts. Pressing the radio on, I reversed out of my forested home in the Dandenong Ranges.

A flurry of early cars passed by. As I waited to merge, I unwound the window, took a deep breath of the crisp morning air. There was an unearthly magic in the surrounding mountain ash forests. Creatures of all kinds dwelled in the shadows, even the sound of the breeze caressing its way through the trees cast a spell over me. When I was young, I was so very positive that I could hear fairies whispering in the treetops.

Turning out, the familiar flashes burst through the pulled drapes of Brennan's house. A photographer, a pretty nice guy who worked all hours on his art. He'd given me a few beautiful nature shots as gifts for running errands for him. He'd had an accident in the past, was now paraplegic and seemed content living in solitude. It seemed such a shame. He young and gorgeous, but never graced the wider world with his presence. I was determined to get him out of the house at some point.

A few kilometres along, I tooted the horn a couple of times outside Jaz's place. I drove right up to the front door. Bellbird song kept my mind from nodding off as I waited... she never came out on time.

I recalled the day Jaz and I met. We first found each other when we were twelve. We'd both started a new school the same day. I'd been home-schooled until then, so hadn't a clue about how to navigate the formidable social terrain of junior high school. Jaz, on the other hand, had been to seven different schools, had three expulsions under her belt, and knew how to establish herself as the top dog in three minutes flat. She was a nightmare, unkempt and foul-mouthed. We had an almost-fistfight on our first meeting at lunchtime. She did the chasing whilst I sent her dizzy circling a tree. That's how we became best friends.

The front door finally opened. Expecting Jaz to come bounding out, I tooted the horn to annoy her, but it was her brother, Ben, ducking under the doorframe. He looked over to me as he headed to the garage. He paused a second, wiped his hands down his work pants and walked over.

"Hey."

"Hey," I replied, fiddling with my lanyard.

"Big day today?" he leaned on my door and smiled. It immediately felt a little warmer.

"Yeah, bit nervous. What about you?"

"Just more of the same. Picked up a nice old Fat Boy to do up."

"A fat what?"

"A Harley, Soph! Picked it up for a song, unfortunately it needs a heap of new parts. We'll have to scale back on the partying."

"Yeah, hard core ravers, aren't we? We'll have to tone down those crazy popcorn-filled movie nights," I said, secretly wishing that wasn't going to happen.

Ben leaned in a little closer. He smelled of grease and spice.

"Maybe I just need to cut back crawling after Jaz. Costs me a fortune ferrying her around," he jutted his chin at the house.

"She'll exhaust herself out eventually. At least you've got me. A hot tea, Netflix binge and I'm sweet. I'm a cheap date." The lanyard snapped. I could have died right there; the earth should have swallowed me whole.

Ben smiled, his chin dimpled, he pushed back from the car. His eyes hooked me just long enough to make me squirm.

"I love those nights, Soph," he said as he stepped away. The space left between us was an unwelcome void.

"Me too,"

Ben tucked his black, shoulder length hair behind his ears and left.

"Catch you later, Soph," he waved, disappearing into the garage to work on this latest motorbike. My cheeks burned whilst he seemed so unaffected, walking away so calm and measured.

You are an utter embarrassment Soph.

Eventually, Tinkerbelle's emo cousin emerged from the house, thankfully interrupting my self-deprecation. Jaz sprayed deodorant on the run. She grumbled her way into the car, cursing to herself about pigs, brothers, and missing clothes.

"Just shows you that genes do count for something. He's such a bloody slob. My scrubs were under his filthy socks," she pretended to gag. "I'm convinced I descend from a more sophisticated heritage. His parents clearly came from Slumland," she rolled her eyes.

"He's not so bad Jaz, just a regular guy, none of them care about clean socks!" I laughed and took the peppermint she offered me every day for 'un-kissable breath.' Jaz remained in a state of half dress, pulling impatiently at her shoelaces and finger-combing her hair.

"Floor it, Soph," she kicked something at her feet. "Oh my God, you too? Is that last week's noodle box? You're a slob, just like him!"

"Again… licence, car, get one. My car, my space!" This was standard character bashing for us, but it was our routine, our love language.

It was a smooth drive down the tree-lined, winding roads, listening to random breakfast radio. Making good time, we detoured for a coffee. Miss Marples was a favourite haunt; the cutest little teahouse on the mountain, with amazing coffee, and scones the size of your head. I'd worked there from age fifteen as a waitress. Alfie and Harriet Fraser were my bosses back then. Alfie currently ran the place on his own since poor Harriet fractured her hip. Being a back of the house handyman, he never looked too comfortable as a barista, but surprisingly made a mean short black. Alfie was a wiry man with a strong Scottish brogue, despite being a forty-year expat. Every kid around here grew up knowing that he was Santa, ringing the bell through the streets of the shire every December. He was brash and loveable; one of a kind.

As we parked, Jaz grumbled about how Ben had spoiled another 'opportunity' the previous night, following her around a nightclub. She didn't understand that he was just watching out for her. Bad boys were her poison. She didn't want to hear me defend Ben, and went inside the café ahead of me, as I grabbed my bag and locked the car.

The back of my neck tingled as I walked through the carpark. A chill slid under my skin. I pulled my handbag closer to my body, quickened my pace. An intrusive, sharp pain fired through my head. The unnerving sensations had me instinctively look over my shoulder, examine every shadow. The café backed onto dense forest; its frontage packed with bountiful gardens... plenty of places to hide. I felt for my phone in my bag, triple zero on my mind, before remembering I'd smashed it an hour ago.

A branch cracked, I spun. A mass of wisteria trailing down the roof of the café shifted, despite the air being perfectly still. Dawn blushed the horizon orange and purple, but night still claimed its place. Everything was too still, not a bird cried. I ran to catch up to Jaz, kept the strange incident to myself, hid my trembling hands in folded arms.

We pushed through glass-panelled doors. The perks of being a former favourite employee meant that I could pop in before opening time to grab a coffee whilst the fresh morning scones were baking.

"Morning, sisters of mercy. Come to cure my ailments?" called a booming voice. He used the same line every single time.

"Morning, Alfie. And no, no one could cure your ails — there are too many. Can we please have the usual?" I asked sweetly.

Jaz whispered sideways in my ear through her teeth.

"If his ails didn't live in a bottle of Glenfiddich, he'd be just fine!"

I elbowed her in the ribs. "Shut up and be nice. He's harmless."

For a girl most would cross the road to avoid, Jaz had some pretty ironic social standards. Alcohol and Jaz didn't mix, she had little tolerance for its use.

The old man with sparse grey hair fumble around at the counter. As ever, Alfie proudly wore a piece of clothing bearing the Fraser family colours.

"No kilt today, Alfie?" I asked.

"Ahh, too nippy for the nether regions these days," he answered in a most matter-of-fact way.

"That's more detail than I needed, but thanks," I made on OMG face at Jaz. She rolled her eyes, disgust clear and present.

Alfie wore a tattered, green and red vest, proudly ironed, with polished silver buttons.

"How's Harriet today?" I asked.

"Oh, she's never better, never better. Especially since your dear old Nan come see 'er. Bless her. She's an angel that woman."

"That she is," I responded as he topped up the coffee grinder.

We waited on a window bench seat out front whilst the intoxicating smell of arabica filled the room. Miss Marple looked down upon us from every direction. A hundred framed photos covered richly papered walls, an homage to the great British mystery sleuth.

"So," Jaz began, "We need a night out in the city. There's a great band playing at a new club on Flinders Lane. I've got to make up for last night. Bloody Ben!"

"Just the two of us?" I asked. "In the city? I don't know, Jaz," Embarrassment clawed up my neck. "I'll stay in, and you know Nan, she's so overprotective."

Yes, yes, I was a young woman in the prime of life, and used to enjoy the odd clubbing experience. I'd just lost interest in the nightlife scene since my last experience. My idea of fun was being outdoors, surrounded by nature. I know that sounds like a tick off the bucket list of a retiree, but I didn't care. It killed Jaz. I was quite sure I was her social faux pas.

"C'mon Soph. Ben will be there… unfortunately for me, fortunately for you. I'm sure his sticky bloody nose will be all over the place. Even though we know he's a pussycat, no one else does. You've seen six-foot six trouble back away from him at a glance. You'll be in good hands. Hopefully, I'll be in hot ones!"

I smacked her leg. "Be nice!"

"Never!" she winked.

I smiled and shook my head, as long as she was safe, what business was it of mine?

"Anyway, you could tell Nan that you're spending the night at my place, a girls' night in." Jaz grabbed my hands. "C'mon Soph, you've got to let your hair down — literally. Have I ever pointed out to you that you never actually wear it down? If you let that rainbow mane down with me by your side, we'll look like Helena Bonham Carter and Barbie on a date! That's action done and dusted!" she laughed wildly at her own joke.

"Jaz, I know you think I'm a geriatric in a twenty-year old's body but…"

"Yes, and your point is?"

"Hmm," I frowned jokingly. "Downtown isn't my thing anymore. All those sweaty bodies squeezed into dark spaces — I can't breathe." I pulled the collar of my shirt to waft in some air. "I'm claustrophobic just thinking about it," I smacked her arm. "And I'm not going to lie to Nan," I eyed her disapprovingly. I was a geriatric.

She rubbed her temples in exasperation. "Sophia, I love Nan, I know she means well — hell, she was right about that last dipstick I dated. But you have to actually live a little, get outside your comfort zone and her shadow. What do you want to do? Go to work, come home, make tea with Nan, and knit your own line of handbags for the rest of your life?" Jaz shrugged her shoulders.

I hugged my handbag to my side in mock shock.

"You can't go to the same two pubs up here for eternity! That's a very small gene pool to dip into. You're young, gorgeous, and never had a boyfriend, girlfriend… whatever your thing is. You seriously don't realise what you're missing out on!" she grabbed my hands as I felt my cheeks burn from the unintended insult.

"You owe yourself a bit of room to take a risk and enjoy yourself. Not everyone's out to get you! There are some nice people out there. I know what happened last June gave you a fright, but that's not representative of every experience," her eyes were sympathetic, though her words were trying to galvanize me into action.

"You're still trying to hook me up! I'm not interested, not just yet," I sighed dramatically. "Unless you can deliver Theo James to my front door, forget it!" I clutched my heart; she rolled her eyes. Jaz needed a partner constantly. She hated quiet, never liked her own company. I was happy to wait for the right one, not just anyone. I never felt the need for constant companionship the way she did. Well, I'd certainly reconsider that stance for Theo, though.

The conversation reminded me of my last experience in central Melbourne. We'd caught a train downtown to the new Docklands development. A boutique club had opened up, and Jaz had managed to procure a few opening night tickets from some poor sap who was after her. Unfortunately for me, Ben was under strict instructions to stay out of her face that night. If he hadn't, my night may have turned out differently.

It had been a nice place, actually. A modern medieval-chic feel, Jaz's taste, down to the finest detail. The crowd looked loaded, and not just with money. Glassy-eyed distant stares surrounded us as bodies moved hypnotically to the reverberating beat under minimalist lighting. It wasn't quite the crowd we were expecting — that kind of partying was totally not our scene. We'd stuck by the bar for a while until, the sap turned up and summoned the guts to ask Jaz to dance. She loved the seductive power she had over people.

"You all right for a while?" she'd asked.

"I'm fine. I'll just be here, admiring the stoners. Try and show some class tonight, Jaz. Just one girl or boy at a time tonight?" I asked, in my best motherly voice.

"Always," she blew a provocative kiss, batted her eyelash extensions and disappeared onto the dance floor.

After a while, a guy in a black hoodie sat next to me and started the usual small talk. Oddly, he stared straight ahead at the mirror behind the bar, not looking in my direction at all. Face shielded by the hood, he seemed underdressed for the place. He picked at a coaster through black gloves.

"You here with anyone?" his voice was strained. He coughed to clear his throat.

The hairs on my neck rose like internal alarm bells. I edged away.

"Yes, actually. My boyfriend is just in the bathroom," my voice wavered with the quick lie.

"Thought you walked in with that chick over there?" he jutted his head in Jaz's general direction.

"My boyfriend is her brother, he brought us in, okay? Look, he'll be back in a minute. I'm not interested, can you please leave me alone?" I'd searched for Jaz, but she was nowhere to be seen.

He stopped talking at that, got up, and walked away with a limp.

Nervous sweat had sprung down my back. This creep has been watching me. The value of having a boyfriend right then seemed to suddenly skyrocket.

My head started to ache, and I felt a little nauseous. I needed some fresh air.

I made my way down a dimly lit hall to find the ladies room, catching my heel on a ripple in the rug. As I bent down to reposition my shoe, a large, gloved hand clapped over my mouth. Whoever it was dragged me out through a door into an internal corridor.

"Don't even think of making so much as a squeak!" the words rumbled cold and wet into my ear.

Immediately, I was sure it was the guy from the bar — his voice was the same. I struggled, twisted and kicked, but I couldn't see him or wrench myself from the iron grip. There was no chance to scream, his hand pressed hard onto my mouth, blood coated my tongue. I fought with all I had, thinking that this was it — I'm going to be tomorrow night's six o'clock news. He dragged me into shadows, pushed me face down onto a concrete floor. He felt me up, all over my back, down my arms and legs. My skin crawled with revulsion, nausea burned my throat, my mind swam. He flipped me over.

"Move and your throat will open like an oyster shell!" Images of all the worst possible things that could happen to a girl in this situation flashed through my mind. My pulse pounded in my ears.

What actually happened though was as terrifying as it was bizarre. He leaned forwards; his face still hidden by the hoodie. His acidic breaths were ragged, laboured; like someone struggling to breathe. He moved with urgency; his head swung around frequently to check that we were alone. He sniffed at the air, like a dog trying to pick up a scent. My limbs froze when he reached for my eyes. I could barely draw a breath; his weight heavy on my chest. I squeezed my eyes closed; my lips trembled wildly. The cold of his gloves pried my left eyelid wide open. His head tilted, face still unseen, inspecting my eyes — for what, I didn't know. He grumbled, seemingly annoyed. His breath was hot and rancid, it gurgled and bubbled. Next came a flash of silver. I struggled for my life then, regardless of his threat. He growled like an animal when I freed an arm, reached up and grasped at the silver weapon with every ounce of my strength. I punched his face, shoving it back into a glimmer of light, immediately wishing that I hadn't. His hood slipped back. A bald, sallow-skinned face with dark, unforgiving eyes glared back. His lips were pale and bloodless, as lifeless as a corpse. I frantically lashed out and registered the coldness of his skin.

He overpowered me again. The weapon slashed at my arm, making sharp, deep contact. A screamed erupted from me. His weight shifted off me. He scrambled up and gazed at his small, scalpel-shaped blade. I shuffled away, taking quick advantage of the freedom. I frantically looked around for an escape route, glanced back at his position, just in time to see him lick my blood off the knife. The bile that had been swirling in my throat ended up on the floor. Limbs a tangled, jellied mess, I tripped over myself, fell against a wall, but managed to explode into a run, expecting another grab to finish me off. Something bright flashed from behind me, it reflected off of the metal door I was yanking open. I looked back momentarily to see my attacker spreadeagled on the floor, a large gash across his head. Dark fluid seeped slowly from the wound. Repulsed, I ran. As the door slammed behind me, I heard a malicious laugh, his voice in my head.

"Now, now, I know who you are. I'll be seeing you real soon, sweet angel. Mmmmm. Yum, yum."

The night was a blur after that. I'd dragged Jaz out and screamed practically the entire way home. It took me two days to tell her what actually happened.

"Soph! Soph? Oh, don't go thinking about that, please? He was just a pervert, high on some kind of dust trying to scare you. He's probably dead or someone's girlfriend in prison by now." Jaz's voice pulled me back from the vile memory.

"Will you at least go somewhere, off the mountain at a minimum, just to get away from here?" she held her arms wide in an exaggerated gesture, indicating the general vicinity around us.

"How about a compromise?" I offered as I pushed the memory far away. "We'll go down to The Mill in The Gully after work tonight to celebrate our first day in the ER. I'm sure the crowd aren't the Neanderthals you think they are."

Her expression brightened slightly at my concession.

"But you have to come for a hike in Sherbrook Forest with me on our next day off together."

"Oh, come on! That's not a fair deal — nature and bugs and ugh," she grumbled. Outdoorsy was not her thing, just like clubs weren't mine. It was a miracle we were even friends.

Thankfully, Alfie interrupted with steaming cups.

"You girls goin' out on the town tonight?" he asked, ever the eaves dropper.

"Yes, Alfie. And yes, I'll mind my manners," I gave him a gentle squeeze on the arm.

"It's those boys who need to mind their manners nowadays. You be sure 'n take that Ben with you; he'll keep their grubby hands off of yer. Yer hear me?" Alfie's eyes sparkled with a little moisture.

"Don't worry yourself, old man. She's a big girl now. We can look after each other. C'mon, Soph. We're going to be late."

Jaz shuffled me out of the front door, the bell tinkering as it opened and closed.

"If you go listening to old McDougall there and his nonsense, you'll end up a spinster, living in a house full of cats!"

"Rude! I like cats,"

I peered back to wave at Alfie, catching him taking a swig from a silver flask hidden under the till.

…continue the series by scanning the QR code.

<u>www.grthomasbooks.com</u>

Thank you for reading The First Satan-Rise of Yeqon.
If you enjoyed this or any other of my stories, please take a moment to
leave a book review on your preferred review platform. Book reviews
are the glitter that make stories shine and are very much appreciated.

Acknowledgements

This story came about as a thank you to my readers who have loved The A'vean Chronicles series and asked for more. The world of A'vean is special to me as they are the first stories that I wrote, the very first I let anyone outside of myself read.

I would like to thank Jas Styles who has been an unrivalled supporter of the A'vean Chronicles and kindly beta read The First Satan for me in its infancy. Thank you Jas for giving your time freely and helping me to flesh out Yeqon's story. You are an angel.

To James and Becky of **Platform House Publishing**, who yet again unfailingly delivered the most stunning book cover and dreamy interior formatting. My books would not be the same without you. Love you both.

Of course, my family are always the greatest of supporters of my writing. They endure my endless anecdotes, inspirational moments, my highs and my lows. Thanks so much fam… love you to bits.

And again, to my readers, just knowing I have taken you away from the mundanity of reality for a moment is the best reward I could ask for.

Thank you again for reading The First Satan-Rise of Yeqon. Your support is forever appreciated.

G.R Thomas

www.ingramcontent.com/pod-product-compliance
Lightning Source LLC
Chambersburg PA
CBHW061122100726
47911CB00013B/650